TH

His ... in, more fl... as his brief, vanishing kisses set off a tumult within her. She ought to have pushed him away. Or boxed his ears. To her amazement, she merely closed her eyes and waited meekly for more.

But there was no more. Instead he pulled away. Harriet's eyes flew open. Bemused, she stared at those sensual lips and wondered why they had abandoned her.

His lips quirked upward in amused satisfaction. Harriet flushed in anger and humiliation. This was precisely what he intended—to demonstrate his masculine power by making her yearn for more.

How insulting that Lord Westwood thought she could be enslaved by such tiny, insignificant kisses. She would show him who was in charge.

She gripped his arm. His smile broadened. Undoubtedly he thought that she meant to beg for another kiss. Harriet parted her lips. She pressed her mouth against his and felt his surprise give way to satisfaction. She nestled closer and felt his hands clench reflexively. She had him now. *He* would beg.

Reforming Harriet

Eileen Putman

A SIGNET BOOK

SIGNET
Published by the Penguin Group
Penguin Putnam Inc., 375 Hudson Street,
New York, New York 10014, U.S.A.
Penguin Books Ltd, 27 Wrights Lane,
London W8 5TZ, England
Penguin Books Australia Ltd,
Ringwood, Victoria, Australia
Penguin Books Canada Ltd, 10 Alcorn Avenue,
Toronto, Ontario, Canada M4V 3B2
Penguin Books (N.Z.) Ltd, 182–190 Wairau Road,
Auckland 10, New Zealand

Penguin Books Ltd, Registered Offices:
Harmondsworth, Middlesex, England

First published by Signet, an imprint of Dutton NAL,
a member of Penguin Putnam Inc.

First Printing, December, 1998
10 9 8 7 6 5 4 3 2 1

Chapter One

LOAF OF LIFE

Elias squinted at the nonsensical name spelled out in cheerfully crooked letters on a sign above the village bakery. From behind the green door wafted the odor of spirits—odd for a bakery on a Sunday morning. The place smelled like a brewery.

Elias trusted his nose, for it had made him rich. It had an unerring ability to sniff out distinctions among pepper berries, detect the subtle aroma of his favorite cassia plant, and judge which coffee beans would appeal to pallid English tastes. He had parlayed the gift of his nose into an uncanny ability to predict the culinary tastes of the times. Coffee, cinnamon, pepper—these formed the foundation of his fortune, gave him a comfortable existence, and kept him far from home.

Though his business—and the military—had taught him that home was wherever a man could spread a pallet, Elias certainly had no desire to spread a pallet anywhere near an establishment that called itself the Loaf of Life. Fortunately, his time in the village would be short.

He knocked on the door and waited expectantly.

The trip to Worthington would not have been necessary had his partner, Lord Frederick Worthington, not had the poor judgment to die, leaving his woefully incompetent widow in charge of the domestic end of the business. It had been the one nasty surprise of an otherwise fortuitous partnership. Freddy had the highest connections in England. Elias had them all over the world. They could have gone on forever, happy as nabobs, thanks to his nose.

No one responded to his knock. Elias tapped his foot impatiently. Through the window, he could see someone moving about. He knocked again.

Elias could not imagine why Freddy had been so stupid as to bequeath his part of the business to his widow, or why the woman's trustees had let her control her own affairs. Then again, Freddy would have done anything to snare a rich wife. Perhaps the crusty Duke of Sidenham, reputed to be something of a hermit but extremely shrewd in his investments, had dictated the terms of Freddy's will as a condition for betrothing his only daughter to a mere viscount. Unfortunately, Freddy had never informed Elias of that fact.

Now Harriet Worthington, or Lady Harriet as she was commonly styled, was fast turning Elias into a pauper.

Which is why, on this May morning that could have been put to better use, Elias's inestimable nose was now pressed against the window of a ridiculously named village shop.

He had already called at Worthington Hall and been informed by a painfully correct butler that her ladyship was not expected for some hours. Hoping to find someone more helpful, Elias had walked down the hill toward the village, but it seemed that all the residents of Worthington were in church this fine Sunday morning. Elias had no intention of venturing *there.* Churches made him uncomfortable.

And so he had strolled through the village, encountering empty shops and shuttered windows until his nose guided him to the bakery and its strong odor of spirits. Whoever worked behind that green door must be thoroughly pickled. Elias knocked once more.

"Open up," he commanded.

Still no response. Elias had no intention of being put off by a drunken baker. As he was weighing whether to give the door a decisive shove, it suddenly swung open—seemingly of its own accord, for no one stood at the threshold. A tingling of alarm shot up the back of his neck. For a moment Elias imagined himself back on the Peninsula, scouting behind enemy lines. He quickly banished that absurd thought, but his senses were nevertheless fully alert as he bent cautiously to accommodate the top of the door frame and stepped into the shop.

"No need to pound," admonished a cheerful voice. "Everyone knows I am here on Sundays. My, you are tall—not that you can help it, of course. Here. Have a petty-patty. Minced veal and cinnamon, though the crust is a bit tough. I worked the dough too long."

Smiling, the woman behind the counter indicated a platter of petit pastries by the door.

Warily, Elias drew nearer. The odor of spirits grew stronger. His lips curled in distaste. The woman must be three sheets to the wind.

Peasant like, a red kerchief covered her hair, though some tendrils had escaped to curl wildly around her cheeks. Her skin was flushed—from drink he supposed, though perhaps it was due to the energetic fashion in which she was working that spongy mass under her hands. A large dot of flour covered the tip of her nose. The corners of her blue eyes crinkled as she regarded him in a friendly fashion. White stuff covered her hands and trailed up to her elbows.

She was, quite simply, a mess.

Elias could not bear unkempt women, though this one might have been comely enough had she not been drunk and wallowing in flour. Her bottle blue eyes held a spirited air, and he suspected she was an entertaining handful between the sheets. She was not *his* type, though. He could not abide disorder or disarray. And she was the very definition of those words.

"I am looking for someone," he began, eyeing the pastries with disdain. There was nothing from this untidy woman's hands he would risk eating. "Perhaps you could be of assistance."

Pursing her lips, she blew an errant tendril away from her face. It floated back onto her cheek, and she pushed it away with the back of her hand, transferring a good deal of the flour to her hair and kerchief.

"Possibly. I know just about everyone in Worthington. Most folks are down at the church. It is just down that path north of the milliner's—"

"I have no desire to visit a church."

"I would be there myself, except that I have promised these pastries to Mrs. Gregory this afternoon. She has her new in-laws visiting and does so want to impress them. Her petty-patties are as good as mine, but she would prefer not to have anything else to worry about, what with Mr. Gregory's temper. Why must some people be so intolerant? Oh, dear!" She put her hand to her face. "I am gossiping to a perfect stranger. Do forgive me."

Elias had no interest in her prattle. He would soon smell like spirits himself if he did not take his leave, and he had no wish to present himself to his new business partner reeking of drink.

"Think nothing of it," he said, schooling himself to patience. "Perhaps you can tell me where I might find Lady Harriet Worthington at this hour."

She gave him an odd look. "Does she know you, sir?"

"Surely that cannot be your concern." Damned if he would open his budget to a tipsy village maid.

"Very well, then." Her tone was noticeably cooler than before. She returned her attention to her dough. In this manner they passed several silent minutes.

An unfamiliar awkwardness filled him. Elias had never

been particularly adept at dealing with females. He suspected he had mishandled matters.

"Perhaps if I might speak to your master, the proprietor?" he suggested amiably. A man would understand. A matter of business, Elias would explain, and Lady Harriet's direction would be his within moments.

Removing her hands from the dough, she wiped them on her apron and lifted her gaze to his. "I have no master," she said evenly. "And that is just the way I like it."

Incredulous, Elias stared at her. "Do you mean to say that this is *your* establishment?"

"Yes. I am my own mistress. Though if one is a woman in such a circumstance, there are always those who disapprove." Her gaze narrowed. "I suspect, sir, that you might be counted in that number."

Taken aback, Elias did not reply. He watched as she cut the dough into little rounds, filled them with a mixture from a bowl, and topped the filling with a thin covering of dough. Brushing the pastries with a yellowish glaze, she popped them into a large oven.

Then she plunged her arms into a pan of water, soaped them up to the elbows, and dried them with a towel. Only then did she remove her kerchief, revealing a gleaming mass of auburn hair under the flour-dusted fabric.

Elias's impatience rapidly transformed into fascination as the woman took off her apron, hung it on a hook near the work counter, and turned to face him. A smattering of flour still adorned her nose, to rather appealing effect, and without that apron he could see that her figure was not in the least coarse. Crossing her arms over her chest, she regarded him with a sharp, clear gaze. She did not look at all tipsy.

"Now, sir," she commanded. "You will be good enough to introduce yourself."

Stung by her authoritative air, Elias refused to allow the woman to seize the upper hand. She was, after all, only a village baker. "And you will remember your manners, girl," he retorted in a tone that usually set underlings to quaking.

"Thank you for reminding me," she said gravely. "I have indeed been remiss. Let me introduce myself: I am the proprietress of the Loaf of Life, a name that reflects my belief that bread is the very companion of the soul. Everything you need to know about me is here in this little shop. I am Harriet Worthington."

Elias's jaw dropped open. "*Lady* Worthington?"

"I prefer to be called Lady Harriet, as I was before my marriage. Since my husband is no longer living, I no longer use his name. I suppose you will think that eccentric."

Elias closed his mouth and regarded her in stunned disbelief.

"Now you really must introduce yourself, sir, and quickly state your business. I have petty-patties in the oven."

"I am Elias Westwood," he managed. "Your late husband's business partner."

She tilted her head. "Lord Westwood—the man who has sent me so many annoying letters of late."

"Which you did not answer," Elias pointed out.

"I never reply to people who purport to tell me what is best for me." She gave him a considering look. "I believe that one must always keep an open mind, my lord. The man who wrote those letters is as closed as any book."

"I beg your pardon," Elias sputtered.

Suddenly, she came from around the counter. "Have a petty-patty," she said, offering the platter to him.

To cover his discomfiture, Elias took a pastry and popped it into his mouth. A heady mixture of veal seasoned with cinnamon sent the most intriguing aroma into his nostrils and tantalized his palate with a fascinating combination of the familiar and exotic. The crust, robust enough to hold the meat but flaky and tender as fine pastry, melted in his mouth.

Heaven had never seen meat pies like these. Elias could not suppress a sigh of pleasure.

"Is everything satisfactory?" Her tone held just a hint of amusement, and Elias hurriedly swallowed the bite and cleared his throat.

"Delicious. My, er, compliments, Lady Harriet. Now, if we might discuss the reason for my visit—"

"Come for tea this afternoon, my lord. I have work to do now." She turned away, a clear dismissal.

Anger rose in his throat. He had had quite enough of this woman's delaying tactics. But an arduously honed discipline forced him to control his fury. He took a deep breath. After all, the village bakery was scarcely the place to conduct his business. A customer might walk in at any moment.

A *customer*? Good God. A duke's daughter was waiting on strangers like a common serving girl. What was going on here? Once more, the heady odor of spirits assailed his nostrils.

"Just exactly what sort of establishment do you run, madam?" he demanded.

She regarded him with a faint air of puzzlement.

"The place smells like a brewery," he explained. Condemnation suffused his tone. Lady Harriet herself might not be drunk, but something was clearly amiss. If ever a woman needed to be taken in hand, it was this one. Elias wondered if Freddy had sanctioned his wife's outlandish behavior.

" 'Tis the yeast, my lord—the barm. I regret that you find it offensive."

"Yeast?"

"I grow my own. In those tubs of ale." She pointed to several dozen crockery jars, lined neatly along one side of the bakery. Noting his disapproval, she added, "Surely you are not one of Dr. Dauglish's disciples?"

"Who?"

"Dr. Dauglish—a pious soul who has set himself up as an expert on baking. He contends that the unfermented loaf is more wholesome, that fermentation indicates decay and corruption. I gather you have not read his treatises?"

A corrupt loaf of bread? Treatises? This conversation was verging on the ridiculous.

"Madam, I could not care less whether your bread is drunk or sober," he declared. "I wish only to settle the business matters between us."

"In that case, come round to the house for dinner. I keep country hours, so you will wish to be early."

"The invitation was for tea," he pointed out uncharitably.

"Yes, but now I think dinner is best." Her attention shifted to the meat pies she was pulling from the oven. Elias could not help but inhale deeply, savoring the wondrous aroma.

"A man deserves a decent meal now and then," she continued. "I sense that your meals have been inadequate, for your disposition is positively bilious."

Looking up, she caught him staring. In fact, he had been damned near salivating over those meat pies. Her eyes twinkled mischievously. Elias turned abruptly and strode to the door.

"Good day, my lord," she called pleasantly.

Elias could not resist a quick look over his shoulder. Lady Harriet was pulling more meat pies from the oven. Furtively, like a spy on a delicate mission, he plucked another pie from the platter and tucked it into his pocket.

It was done quickly, with no one the wiser—he thought.

But the sound of her soft laughter followed him out into the street.

Harriet put the finishing touches on her toilette. Her maid, Heavenly, shook her head in disapproval. "If you ask me, them that want to soften up a man ought to pretty the package a bit."

"I will not cater to that man's twisted notions of femininity," Harriet declared. Indeed, she was quite satisfied with her appearance. Her hair, normally as unruly as a basket of yarn the cats had got into, was pulled severely off her face and rolled into a little bun at the nape of her neck. She had deliberately chosen one of her severest dinner gowns, a high-necked black bombazine with long sleeves. She was ready to do battle.

Lord Westwood's sudden visit had been a most unwelcome surprise. For months she had ignored his letters and their increasingly strident tone. She had thought him safely tucked away on one of those islands Freddy had spoken about, and the last thing in the world she had expected was to find him in her shop this morning.

"You don't look like yourself, Miss Harriet," Heavenly insisted. "And when a woman don't look like herself, she don't act like herself. And when she don't act like herself, she—"

"Spare me another of your lectures, Heavenly. I am perfectly myself. Why, who else would I be?" Harriet laughed, though in truth she was a little nervous. Lord Westwood had not been at all as she had expected.

She had imagined a man who wrote such disapproving letters to be a prissy sort, small and bespectacled, balding and pinch-mouthed. But Lord Westwood was large—he had had to stoop to enter her shop—and much younger than she had envisioned. Indeed, his vigorous appearance put him in the very prime of life. His sun-burnished skin suggested he had spent many of his days outdoors, though she could not imagine a man of his hauteur actually working the fields. No doubt he employed slaves to perform the labor. Alas, she had heard that many of the plantations did, despite the reforms forged by Mr. Wilberforce and others.

Lord Westwood looked to be the type of man to use another human being in such a despicable fashion. His eyes were exceedingly hard. More black than blue, they conjured the dark, unforgiving void of a soul locked in endless isolation.

Did the man never smile? She doubted that arrogant mouth was capable of mirth. In many ways, Lord Westwood looked to be the very opposite of Freddy, for Freddy had certainly enjoyed a good laugh. Had he been laughing, she wondered idly, when he collapsed and died in the arms of Lady Forth?

"Hand me that shawl, Heavenly, if you please."

"Miss Harriet, you need a shawl like you need another loaf of bread. Any more fabric on those shoulders and you'll suffocate."

Harriet ignored the warning, as she had been ignoring Heavenly's axioms for the majority of her twenty-four years. The shawl gave her something to hold onto, a bit of extra security. The thought of entertaining Lord Westwood for dinner had, as the day wore on, brought grave misgivings.

Oh, she would hold her own—she had done so with men for years. What bothered her was the prospect of spending an evening in his forbidding company unrelieved by the welcome distraction of others. Guests were as necessary to a meal as yeast to bread. Harriet rarely dined alone. Never alone with a man.

"I wish I had invited Squire Gibbs. Or the Tanksleys," she murmured half to herself.

"Squire would spend the evening trying to get that mill away from you, and Mrs. Tanksley would go on and on again about why you should marry her son," Heavenly muttered.

"Well, I do not intend to sell the mill, and I certainly do not intend to marry, so that is that."

Harriet swept down the grand staircase that had been one of Freddy's proudest accomplishments. He had ordered the pink marble from Italy and the gold from Africa and had craftsmen from Ireland apply the gilt to the mahogany railing carved by Thomas Sutterly, one of the country's foremost wood-carvers. Harriet had never seen anything half as grand, even in her father's house. Personally, she thought the carvings of naked angels twining up the banister a bit much. But she had always believed in tolerance. If one could not accept a husband's eccentricities, one could hardly be considered tolerant.

Downstairs, Harriet checked the table arrangements, though it was unnecessary—Horace knew her tastes precisely and always followed them to the letter. Her quick trip into the kitchen was likewise fruitless, as Celestial had everything well in hand. Heavenly and Celestial had been employed in her father's household for as long as she could remember and had joined her staff upon her marriage to Freddy—though perhaps "joined" was the wrong word for two such strong-willed women. Actually, they had invaded the household, giving Horace fits in the process. Freddy had been appalled by the easy familiarity Harriet enjoyed with the twins, but then Freddy had been a bit of a snob.

Harriet suspected that Lord Westwood had more than a touch of the snob in him. The man's nose looked positively regal, and he carried himself like the nabob he was. No doubt he lived like a king, with all the trappings that wealth could provide.

Wealth, Harriet had found, meant very little in the overall scheme of things. Her father was as rich as Croesus, but her enormous dowry had been woefully unable to purchase wedded bliss. Freddy had piddled away most of her funds on his gilt banisters and gilded women. She had been surprised as anyone to find herself part owner of a West Indies shipping concern, but what did any of it matter? Money was not the measure of a man—or woman.

Unfortunately, she was doomed to spend an evening with Lord Westwood discussing that very subject, for the man's letters had been rife with talk of profits, loss, capital, investments. Apparently he meant for her to consult him on every business move. The more Harriet thought about it, the more she resented the intrusion upon her time that this evening would mean.

But when Horace ushered Lord Westwood into the drawing room, her resentment faded. The man looked magnificent. The black superfine fit his broad shoulders with nary a hint of padding. His white breeches hugged his well-formed calves like a second skin. A cravat, tied in some exotic but restrained style, framed his chin and set off his dark features to gleaming perfection. His tousled black hair graced his high forehead with natural ease and with none of the dandy's conceit or artificiality.

He smiled slightly. His parted lips revealed fine, straight teeth and, unbelievably, a hint of a dimple in one cheek. Without a disapproving look upon his face, Lord Westwood was devastatingly handsome.

Harriet steeled herself against the unsettling effect of that unexpected smile. No doubt he intended to charm her into signing over Freddy's part of the business.

"Good evening, Lady Harriet."

"Good evening, Lord Westwood," she replied coolly, suddenly feeling most inadequate in her black bombazine.

How excruciatingly polite and formal they were, especially when earlier he had seen her covered with flour. She extended her hand. He brushed it lightly with his lips, then held onto it rather longer than necessary as he seated himself in the chair next to hers. Horace poured sherry and discreetly left the room.

Harriet decided not to mince words. "You should know at the outset, my lord, that I have no intention of selling my part of the business to you. Nor do I intend to consult you on decisions I make regarding my investments."

The polite smile faded from his face. "How is it, madam," he said in a constricted voice, "that you possess such an extraordinary amount of freedom in the matter?"

"My father is the sole trustee of my inheritance. For reasons he has chosen to keep to himself, he has allowed me to do as I wish." Probably so that he would not have to be bothered with her, Harriet thought resentfully.

"Freddy had no heir?"

"Not one that has been found. It is a worthless title, at all events. There is no entail now—thanks to Father's machinations. I inherited everything."

"I see." He was silent for a moment. "The business has lost a great deal of money since Freddy's death."

"If I have been responsible for that—"

"You have."

"—I apologize, but I am sure that the loss of a few pounds has not seriously altered your affairs."

"Sixty thousand."

"I beg your pardon?"

"Sixty thousand," he repeated. "The decisions I have been unable to implement because of your refusal to respond to my instructions have resulted in the loss of sixty thousand pounds since November last. A king's ransom, madam."

Harriet hesitated. It was rather a formidable sum. She had not kept track, for such things did not concern her. Still, Lord Westwood looked as if he could stand the loss of quite a bit more without being beggared.

"I assure you that my part of the business has been engaged in good works. I sold some of the stock to pay for the Whitmires' wheat crop, which was devastated by the rains last year. Now they can plant winter wheat, which many think is actually a superior grain and—" Harriet broke off. Lord Westwood looked dangerously apoplectic.

"You sold stock in Westwood Imports to pay for a neighbor's wheat crop?" he demanded, thunderstruck.

"There was also Mrs. Filbert's cow, which died suddenly last month," Harriet said a bit defensively. "A family cannot subsist without a cow."

"A cow," he echoed.

"And the mill needed to be rebuilt. Squire did not keep it up, and Freddy had done no repairs after winning it in that card game. The people depend on the mill. And before the mill could be useful, we had to tear down the old dam, which was diverting the water power by flooding an old pasture. But the Reeds needed water to irrigate their fields, so we built a new dam just below the mill, and everyone is quite happy now. Especially the Smythes, who owned the old swampy pasture. Now they can use it for grazing land. Of course they did not have any grazing animals until—"

"You bought them a herd of sheep."

Harriet beamed. "How did you know?"

Lord Westwood exhaled slowly. "Lady Harriet," he began in a patient tone, "I am certain that your neighbors are grateful for your assistance. But you have succeeded in severely depleting the assets of a business which I founded, which bears my name, which until last fall was extremely productive—without consulting me. Do you think that is fair?"

"When you put it that way, my lord, perhaps not. But I suspect you had too much money to begin with."

He blinked in amazement, and Harriet rushed on. "The business never did Freddy any good, you know. He had a most unfortunate gambling habit and frittered away his money on unhealthy pursuits. I believe, in fact, that your business hastened his death."

"Whatever pursuits in which your husband was engaged," he said through gritted teeth, "it is hardly fair to take your anger at him out on my business—"

"Oh, I am not angry," Harriet assured him. "Not at all. Freddy was entitled to do as he wished. But he could not handle wealth, and I believe it shortened his life."

"So you decided to give the wealth away."

Harriet smiled. "Just so, my lord. I believe it has been put to good use."

Lord Westwood rose, his features rigid. "I thank you for the sherry," he said in a tight voice, "but I cannot stay for dinner. I am having great difficulty controlling my temper. We will talk on another occasion."

"Oh, dear," said Harriet. "And I had Celestial prepare broiled salmon with caper sauce."

He paused. "Caper sauce?"

Harriet nodded. "I find it marries quite beautifully with the raspberry vinegar marinated asparagus—though one might be forgiven for assuming that the pungent flavors would do battle. They do not, I assure you."

"I suppose you cook the life out of it." He set his glass on the table with a thump.

"The asparagus? Oh, no, sir. We steam it, just until the color turns. Then we plunge the stalks into cold water to stop the cooking. They are wonderfully crisp and more than hold their own with my crusty French rolls. And the buttered prawns are spiced with plenty of garlic, so as not to fade away amid the other dishes. I like food that makes one sit up and take notice."

With a deep breath, Lord Westwood squared his shoulders. "I am sure it is delicious, and I regret ruining your dinner, but I have learned over the years that my temper is not to be trifled with. I am afraid I must—"

"Trifle? Oh, dear, you just reminded me!" Harriet rose.

"I have made a marvelous trifle for dessert—an international dish, actually. English custard spread over a cake soaked in Madeira wine, garnished with candied fruits from the Indies. I top it with ice cream flavored by Turkish apricots. But if you are not staying for dinner, I must tell Celestial not to unmold the ice cream, else it will be ruined. Please excuse me."

As she moved toward the door, Lord Westwood cleared his throat.

"Lady Harriet." His voice sounded strained.

"Do not worry," she assured him. "I am not offended by your premature departure. I have a most open mind about masculine behavior."

"It is just that I would hate to . . ." He looked uncomfortable.

"Yes, my lord?" Harriet said encouragingly. Lord Westwood was an extremely difficult man to read.

"I would hate to ruin your trifle."

"Oh." Harriet frowned in confusion. "Does that mean you wish to stay for dinner after all?"

But before he could answer, the door opened and Horace stood at the threshold. "Dinner is served," he intoned.

The aromas of freshly broiled salmon, caper sauce, raspberry vinegar, garlic, and exotic fruits filled the room. Lord Westwood took another deep breath, pulled out a handkerchief, and wiped his brow. He closed his eyes.

"Yes," he declared in a ragged tone, "I believe I do."

Chapter Two

His nose had betrayed him. Elias had been ready to walk out of Lady Harriet's parlor, taking his rage safely into the night before it brought disaster. But his nose had sabotaged his plans, and now he sat at her table, consoling his anger with raspberry vinaigrette and capered salmon.

A rich fish like salmon deserved a zesty accompaniment. Most cooks never understood that. Harriet Worthington did. She also knew how the lush, pink meat should be cooked—just until the edges lightened, leaving a deep band of pink inside.

"Otherwise it dries out," she told him. There was no need to explain to Elias. He had been eating salmon for years. He hated it dried and meaty like worn-out beef. Lady Harriet might be an abysmal businesswoman, but she was the first hostess he had met who truly understood salmon.

"I quite agree," he found himself saying, before he remembered that she was the enemy, the woman singlehandedly depleting his fortune and turning his business into an agrarian charity.

But as he stared at the trifle and the thick topping of sumptuous ice cream, Elias knew he would not regain his common sense until this heady experience of taste and smell was behind him, until Lady Harriet rose and declared the dinner over and he could prevail upon her to continue the discussion in more neutral territory.

Someone with the improbable name of Celestial had prepared the food, but Lady Harriet had obviously supervised every dish. Elias could not help but admire a woman with such skill. Though she had swathed herself in black bombazine—a concession to mourning, perhaps, though Freddy had been dead a full year—he tried to imagine how she would look in a more revealing gown. A gown that, like the Turkish apricots adorning that luscious ice cream, complemented a distinctively sensual essence.

In the bakery her reddish-brown hair had formed an appealing tangle of curls. Tonight it was tamed into an unflattering bun that might have looked sleek and elegant on another woman but which seemed incongruous on someone accustomed to plunging her hands into flour up to her elbows. Duke's daughter or no, Lady Harriet was not a woman he would have described as elegant. She had an earthier appeal, as if she knew what it was to run barefoot in the meadow, hair blowing out from her flushed face, blue eyes reflecting the glory of a clear sky.

To be sure, there was nothing coarse about her. Even in that flour-dusted frock, she had carried herself with quiet assurance, her eyes reflecting a calm self-possession. But something niggled at him, something that hinted of hidden currents beneath those still waters.

What had she said? That she was her own mistress, that Freddy had been entitled to do as he wished, that she had a "most open mind" about masculine behavior. Slowly, Elias began to suspect a startling truth about Lady Harriet's marriage.

Whatever "unhealthy pursuits" in which Freddy had been engaged—and Elias could guess at some of them—Lady Harriet had sanctioned them because it suited her to do so, perhaps because she wished to enjoy a similar freedom. His eyes narrowed assessingly. Under that dreadful bombazine and constricted bun was a woman who understood the essence of appetites. He wondered how many lovers she had had.

For the first time it occurred to him that there might be a way around his difficulty with her. He inhaled again, savoring the fine Madeira bouquet. There was only one way to tame a woman like Lady Harriet, and he suspected Freddy had not had the means or resolve to do it. Of the two partners in Westwood Imports, Elias had always been the one to make the hard decisions and to execute them ruthlessly.

Lady Harriet needed a firm hand—*his* hand. He would school her to his touch, much as he would bring a highly strung filly to the bit. Once he had bedded her, she would dance to his tune. Unlike Freddy, he would brook no nonsense. She would make a fine mistress.

It would not do to trip the snare too soon, though. As with any recalcitrant target, he would have to exercise subtlety. Elias placed his napkin on the table. "I do not know when I have had a more delicious meal."

"Thank you." She looked wary, as if she distrusted compliments. He would have to remember that.

"Would you favor me with a turn in the garden?" he asked smoothly. "A rich meal ought to be followed by a pleasant bit of exercise."

When she did not immediately respond, Elias frowned in consternation. He knew little about the finer arts of persuasion. Women either fell into his lap or they did not. This one had apparently decided to make things difficult. "You might call your maid to accompany us if the notion makes you uncomfortable," he suggested, although that was the last thing he wanted.

She gave him a tentative smile. "Heavenly would jump at the chance, but I do not think I need a chaperone. It is just that I must rise very early tomorrow to see to things at the bakery. I confess I am rather tired. But, come. Let us take the night air. The garden is very lovely."

Elias did not know who Heavenly was, but he was not about to have his future mistress regularly stoking the fires of the village bakery. "Most women of your station do not occupy themselves in such pursuits," he observed as she led them out of the house and past a stoned-lined flower bed to the terrace.

"Yes, I know. My friend Mrs. Tanksley is forever telling me so." Beyond the terrace, lanterns illuminated a path that opened into a large, sprawling garden. Elias could just make out a profusion of erect green plants that emitted a wondrous scent.

"Mint," he pronounced, letting the pleasurable smells fill him. "And savory. A bit of thyme over in that direction, some rosemary under that ornamental cherry."

Amazed, she stared at him. "Are you a gardener, my lord?"

"I merely have a heightened sense of smell. It has been useful in my business."

"I see." She regarded him with interest. "You identified my herbs perfectly. Celestial planted most of them, along with a few others I cannot name that she believes capable of curing various ailments. I confess that my own knowledge of herbs is rather limited."

Elias met her gaze and disciplined himself to ignore the limpid blue softness there. "You have not answered my question about the bakery. Is it not untoward to involve oneself in such a lowering occupation?"

Her expression tightened as she led him onto the path. "Bread carries the staff of nourishment. There is nothing lowering about bringing its diverse elements together in glorious harmony for the good of the soul."

Elias shot her a sidelong glance. Most assuredly, Lady Harriet was short a sheet. He hoped that would not affect her skill between the sheets. "Making bread for the household is one thing," he conceded. "But running a bakery is commerce, and commerce is not for gently bred females. Surely, Freddy did not allow you to engage in such activities while he was alive."

She halted so suddenly that Elias nearly ran into her. "I never presumed to tell my husband what to do, and he never presumed to tell me," she said coolly. "We had an egalitarian marriage. I see no more reason to restrict my behavior as a widow than I did as a wife."

Yes, Elias decided, the Duke of Sidenham must have extracted monstrous promises from Freddy in exchange for Lady Harriet's hand. He could not imagine any other reason a husband would allow his wife such outlandish freedom.

"I did not intend to pry," he parried. "You are still in mourning for your husband. I am sorry."

"I was never in mourning," she retorted. "I do not believe in mourning the dead when one should be celebrating the living."

"You wear black," he pointed out, beginning to think himself lost in a maze in which every corner opened into a thicket of thorns.

Lady Harriet looked down at her dress. "Oh, this. This was for you."

Elias stared at her.

"Silly of me, was it not? I did not want to appear too . . . too feminine." Her cheeks took on an appealing color that might have been a blush—or only the lantern's flickering light.

A strange warmth stole over him as well. "Might as well tell the sun not to shine," he heard himself reply—to his utter amazement.

Her little gasp surprised him. Now he had no difficulty making out the scarlet on her face. Her tentative smile sent a tiny, unexpected thrill coursing through his veins.

Where had those words come from? He did not normally play the gallant. Elias cleared his throat. "I apologize. I did not mean to seem familiar."

"Not familiar," she corrected. "Only too flattering. I am afraid I never learned the art of flirtation. I am quite comfortable in large groups, but I do not seem to know how to entertain a solitary gentleman."

It was on the tip of his tongue to suggest a number of possibilities, but Elias kept his mouth shut. Neither the military nor the business world had taught him how to ingratiate himself with females who possessed Lady Harriet's unnerving independence. And though he was accustomed to expressing his wishes and having them obeyed, he knew such bluntness would never work with this woman.

"As to that," he said at last, "you have entertained me quite thoroughly." He managed a chivalrous smile and was rewarded by seeing her blush once more.

Elias was not a patient man; he did not intend to take forever to charm Lady Harriet into complying with his wishes. But he could afford to bide his time for a bit.

Besides, being in her company was not an onerous chore. The caper sauce alone was worth it.

"Now, Squire, we have covered this ground. I have no intention of selling you the mill." Exasperated, Harriet pushed her hair back from her face with the back of her hand, the only part that was not covered in flour. It was just like Cedric Gibbs to show up when she was distracted by the demands of her new sourdough culture.

"But, Harriet," he protested, "Freddy never meant to keep the thing. He was to offer me a chance to buy it back at the first opportunity. Had he not died so suddenly—"

"Nevertheless he did, and he never said a word to me about returning the mill to you. You had let it sink into the most deplorable state, whereas I am happy to make the necessary repairs. It is much better off in my hands. The people need a working mill."

Fury rose in Cedric's florid face. The man was not much above forty, but, like his mill, had let himself deteriorate. He was overly fond of drink and with his grating disposition had managed to offend just about everyone in Worthington at one time or another.

Monica Tanksley insisted that losing the mill to Freddy had improved Cedric's character. He *had* been rather amiable lately, but Harriet suspected it was all for show. The squire's family had controlled the mill for decades and made a fortune by charging people enormous sums to grind their grain. Though Harriet now allowed him to use the mill for a nominal sum—as she did all her neighbors—she knew he would not be satisfied until the mill returned to his ownership.

His latest tactic was to try to woo her for it. He had not yet worked himself up to an offer, but it was only a matter of time. His sudden appearance in the bakery this morning, when she was alone, did not bode well.

"Please excuse me," Harriet said. "I have work to do."

"*My* work has become considerably lighter without my mill," he responded acidly.

"And a great deal less profitable," she could not refrain from noting, "since you are not able to charge three times the going rate for milling."

Cedric regarded her through narrowed eyes. His late wife, God rest her, had been as eager to please as a good sheepdog. She did not run on at the mouth like a man, nor had she criticized him. She had birthed him ten children, eight of whom survived, and it had been much easier to feed them all when he had the mill. He did not see how Lord Worthington had tolerated being in the same house with his shrewish wife. But Cedric swallowed his own biting retort in favor of a more agreeable one.

"With all due respect, Harriet, you have not lived in

this community for a lifetime. I have always been considered a fair man. Anyone who could not pay their shot had no trouble finding credit with me."

"For triple interest," she pointed out.

Again, Cedric held his temper. He knew he would have to tolerate her gibes until he got her into his bed. So far, she had shown no sign of succumbing, but Harriet had been a year without a man. A man was necessary for pleasure, for happiness. She needed him, or someone like him, and there was no one else around at the moment. Monica Tanksley had been trying to match Harriet up with her son Eustace, but young Eustace was a mere pup.

Cedric could give her a ready-made family. Eight children—a bit unruly, but only because they lacked a mother's touch. His Hilda had been gone for four years. He needed a wife. With Harriet's money and the only working mill for fifteen miles, he would be a king. Some might think her a bit above his touch, but the Gibbs name was good enough for a dowager viscountess who had sunk so low as to open her own bread shop.

"I would certainly consider your suggestions for revising my fees," Cedric said magnanimously.

Harriet scarcely heard him. She was pondering the bubbling sourdough culture, wondering how long the Egyptians had allowed the smelly mixture to stand before deeming it ready to use. It was one of her missions to experiment with new breads. Lady Hester Stanhope, with whom she had developed a friendship several years ago in London, had recently sent her several dried cultures from the Middle East. Harriet's first attempt to produce a good Egyptian sourdough had resulted in a bricklike loaf unsuitable for anything but the crows. But she was determined to succeed. It would be nice to serve something special tomorrow night, when the Tanksleys and Lord Westwood were coming to dine.

Lord Westwood seemed to appreciate adventurous

cooking. To be sure, he was a thoroughly annoying man, but she had found herself softening toward him last night. His flattery had been outlandish, but she might forgive the excesses of a man caught up in the afterglow of a good meal.

So intent was Harriet's concentration that she did not realize Cedric had slipped around the counter until his large hand clamped down on her shoulder and startled her into a little shriek.

"Now, Harriet," he said in a soothing tone, "there is no need to be coy. I know how lonely a bed can be."

"You will remove your hand from my person," Harriet ordered firmly, though in truth his precipitous advance alarmed her. Harriet had risen early so as to have the bakery to herself this morning; the other women would not arrive for another hour. She and Cedric were completely alone.

Acting as if he had not heard, Cedric pulled her into an embrace. Harriet cringed. The man's breath would have felled an oak. "Stop it, sir, this instant!"

"No need to play the reluctant virgin, Harriet," he assured her. "You have been a married lady. You can trust me with your deepest desires."

"My deepest desire, Cedric, is that you remove yourself from my shop." Harriet tried to back away, but he had trapped her against the counter. Frantically, she fumbled behind her, searching for anything that might serve as a weapon. Just as her fingers found the bowl containing the new culture, she heard the door scrape open.

"What the devil is going on here?"

Harriet instantly recognized the deep voice. "Lord Westwood!" she squeaked, greatly relieved.

Cedric took one look at the tall figure looming at the shop entrance and immediately released her. Unfortunately, Harriet had bent back so far over the counter that when his arms fell away, she lost her balance. She tumbled to the floor in an ungainly heap.

In one smooth motion, Lord Westwood vaulted over the counter, pulled her to her feet, and slammed Cedric against the wall. "You struck her," he growled.

"No, no!" Harriet cried. "It was not like that, my lord!"

Her words made the earl turn, which allowed Cedric the opportunity to vent his displeasure at the manner in which his captor's hands gripped his throat. The squire leveled a blow at Lord Westwood's jaw.

Cursing in pain, Lord Westwood grabbed Cedric by the collar and yanked him off his feet. Cedric responded by kicking the earl in the knee. With animal-like snarls, the two men launched themselves at each other.

"Oh, dear!" Harriet watched in dismay as they slammed against the counter, sending bread pans clattering to the floor.

"Stop it!" she cried, but neither man paid her any mind. Harriet feared for the fate of her shop unless they could be separated, but their savage expressions suggested that neither man would listen to reason.

Without a moment's hesitation, Harriet reached for the crock containing the sourdough culture and threw the contents over the two combatants.

Both men roared in outrage, then instantly separated, which almost—but not quite—compensated for the loss of her precious culture.

"What the devil!" thundered Cedric. He uttered a series of curses, then stomped out from behind the counter like an enraged bull. His hands came up but froze midway to her neck as he struggled for control. Glaring at her with an expression of pure fury, he marched out into the street, slamming the door behind him as the thick culture dripped from the back of his jacket. Cedric had not gotten the worst of it, however. That privilege belonged to the earl, whose head and shoulders were covered with the stuff.

Lord Westwood stood perfectly still, as if he could not believe what had occurred. Quickly, Harriet handed him a dish towel. Without saying a word, he took it and began to wipe the pasty culture from his eyes. The pungent odor, which was to have imparted such a wonderful taste to her bread, brought a revolted expression to his features.

"What is this putrid substance?" he said in a voice of deadly calm.

Too calm, Harriet thought nervously, recalling what he had said about his temper. "An Egyptian bread culture," she explained. "I was hoping to use it to bake a special bread for dinner tomorrow night."

Lord Westwood did not reply. Carefully, he began to apply the towel to his head, although the fetid residue clung to his thick hair like glue. It was a hopeless task, and nothing less than a total dunking in a hot bath would repair the damage. She supposed he was staying at the Boar's Head Inn, which was not known for hot baths—or *any* baths, the proprietor being notoriously stingy.

Harriet could not imagine Lord Westwood presenting himself at the inn in such condition.

"It is still early," she ventured. "There is scarcely anyone about yet. Perhaps you would like to come back to the house with me. I will ask Horace to prepare a bath. No one in Worthington would be any the wiser, and you would not have to be seen until you repaired your appearance."

The rigid set of his jaw told her that slinking into her house for a bath was the last thing he wished to do. But he must also have seen that it was the only way.

"Yes," he said at last.

Harriet waited for something else—a snarled reproach, a scathing denunciation, perhaps. But he merely stood silently, keeping himself in check, as she moved quickly toward the door.

"The gig is just out front." Harriet forced a cheerful tone to her voice, in spite of a sinking feeling of dread. Lord Westwood looked like a man ready to explode. She did not want to be around when he did.

"Thank you," he said softly. "Thank you very much."

Chapter Three

Elias did not trust himself to speak. He remained silent during the ten minutes it took the gig to travel to Lady Harriet's home. And during the fifteen minutes he stood in her foyer as servants hurried to heat water for his bath. And during the entire time he remained in his fetid clothes, his hair coated with the stinking goo that evidently was part of Lady Harriet's culinary magic.

His dignity suffered mightily, for though most well-trained servants would have gone about their business without remarking upon his appearance, these people apparently enjoyed excessive familiarity with their employer. The woman Lady Harriet called Heavenly quickly fetched another servant from the kitchen. Putting their hands over their mouths to stifle their laughter, the two women stared at him for the longest time. Only the butler maintained some decorum, but it did not take a genius to read the mirthful gleam in the man's eye.

Gritting his teeth, Elias tried to suppress his rage and chagrin. The woman he had thought to seduce—indeed, to rule—had turned him into an object of abject ridicule. He stood before her as a fetid specimen of humanity, never to regain the ground lost to odoriferous indignity.

He wanted to strangle her.

"This way, my lord," Lady Harriet said in the cheerfully cajoling tone one might use with a recalcitrant child.

Elias followed her up the ridiculously ornate staircase

and into a room that held a large copper hip bath. Steam warmed his nostrils invitingly. Staring at the enormous tub, he knew a faint glimmer of hope.

"Horace will fetch your clean clothes from the inn," she said. "I gather you are not traveling with a valet?"

What he would not give to place himself in Henry's capable hands. But he had seen no need for the batman to accompany him on an errand that was to have occupied only a brief afternoon. Consequently, Henry was in London, enjoying a respite from his duties and doubtless draining his employer's stock of French brandy.

"No," Elias bit out.

"Then Horace will serve in his stead. He has laid out a dressing gown for your immediate comfort, but you may be assured that he will return with your clothes as quickly as he can." She paused. "Unless you wish him to stay and assist you in the bath?"

"I can manage my own damned bath."

"Yes, of course." Hastily, she backed out of the room.

With a sense of desperation, Elias ripped off his clothes and plunged into the steaming tub. He ducked his head under the water and let it wash away the morning's indignities.

To be sure, he was not entirely blameless in the matter. Knowing her intention to work at the bakery this morning, he had risen early from his bed at the inn and hurried to the shop to catch her unawares—and perhaps receptive to whatever charm he possessed—only to find that a lecherous country squire had formed the same notion.

Sliding the soap over his skin, Elias detected the scent of lime—with a hint of cinnamon, of all things—and wondered wildly if Lady Harriet's soap was edible. Even the soap in this household did wondrous things to his senses. As he let the comfortable oblivion of his bath sweep him, Elias could not help but realize how difficult his task was now. If Lady Harriet was the regular recipient of boorish advances like the one he had witnessed this morning, she would not welcome anything remotely similar from him.

Damnation. He wished he could carry the woman off and be done with it. Once in his bed, she would see things his way. His business would be his again.

But after today she might always see him as the stinking spectacle who had stood dripping and disgusting in her foyer. Even after he was bathed and respectable again, she might have to work to hide her laughter—as her servants had hid guffaws behind their open palms.

He did not stand a chance at seduction.

Harriet had caught the merest glimpse of Lord Westwood's bare back as he plunged into the bath. She could not help it; the door was not fully closed when he ripped off his clothes. And though she ought to have been mortified, gratified more accurately described her feelings as she tiptoed away down the hall.

His well-tailored clothing concealed an amazing display of masculine musculature. Though she would never tell a soul that she had been so shameless as to peek, the image would stay with her for a long, long time.

Freddy had not possessed rippling muscles. His were wasted by inactivity and debauchery, and no one knew better than she how he had squandered his resources, masculine and otherwise. Harriet had not held that against him—she liked to think of herself as without prejudice—but she had not known there were such men as Lord Westwood for comparison.

"I do hope your bath was restorative," she murmured an hour later as she poured out coffee for his breakfast. The sideboard was laden with ham, kidneys, eggs with nutmeg sauce, and fresh bread. Harriet hoped the meal would help mollify him; he never would have eaten so well at the Boar's Head Inn.

Lord Westwood accepted the coffee without a word. When she asked whether she could fill his plate, he nodded his assent. Though his silence was disconcerting, Harriet told herself he simply preferred to concentrate on his food.

His hair still bore a faint sheen of moisture from his bath. In his fresh burgundy jacket with fawn trousers, he looked like a typical country gentleman finishing off a deeply satisfying breakfast. Indeed, he ate everything she set before him. But when he placed his napkin on the table and met her gaze, he looked anything but satisfied.

"Has that man struck you before?" he asked quietly.

"Squire Gibbs?" Harriet eyed him in surprise. "Oh, goodness no, my lord. You mistook the situation. I merely fell because he released me so abruptly."

"You were struggling with him."

"Yes, but I was not afraid—" Harriet broke off. She *had* been afraid, a little. Though she had known Cedric Gibbs for years, in recent months he had become rather desperate in the matter of the mill.

Lord Westwood arched a skeptical brow. "Surely, you do not wish me to believe that you welcomed his advances? That his appearance in the shop this morning was expected?"

"Certainly not!" Harriet replied indignantly. "I do not arrange rendezvous with men in my bakery. Or anywhere, for that matter," she quickly added. "Anyway, Cedric does not want *me*. He wants to buy back the mill Freddy won from him during a card game. He has exhausted all verbal means of persuasion, and I believe he has the misguided notion that if he seduces me, I will give him what he seeks. Despicable scheme, is it not?"

Lord Westwood coughed into his napkin.

"Some men cannot get it into their heads that women are better off without them," she added.

"Are they?"

"Oh, yes. But you will be thinking me disrespectful of Freddy. I am not glad he is gone, my lord, but I have managed to get along quite well by myself."

"This morning was proof of that, of course."

Was that odd note in his voice sarcasm? "I was grateful for your assistance, Lord Westwood," Harriet said quickly. "I have not thanked you properly."

"You have done more than enough, madam."

This time, Harriet had no trouble recognizing the sarcasm. She flushed. "I am sorry about the sourdough culture. I was simply trying to stop the scuffle while my shop was still in one piece."

"I understand perfectly." His thunderous expression and the sardonic edge to his voice belied his words.

Harriet knew she had earned his anger. It was not the first time her brain had failed to think through the disastrous ramifications of her actions. She ought to have learned something from that very first disaster—her marriage to Freddy—but she had only grown more impulsive since then, not less. "I cannot say again how sorry I am, my lord. Is there anything I can do to make it up to you?"

"Sell me the remaining shares of my business."

Taken aback, Harriet met his gaze. There was no hint of humor there. "You are very blunt, my lord."

"I like to put my cards on the table."

"Very well. I will be frank, too. The shares are mine, and I intend to keep them to help the people of this community as their needs arise."

He made an impatient sound. "I will pay you well. Use the money to buy cows, or pigs, or anything you like."

"It is not the same."

"Damnation, woman," he growled. "You are selling off my business for a pittance. And whoever is brokering the transactions is probably stealing you blind, having long ago figured out that you do not have the slightest idea what your shares are really worth."

"Mr. Stevens was Freddy's solicitor," Harriet protested. "I am sure he must be honorable."

"Freddy's solicitor?" Lord Westwood gave a scornful laugh. "Now *there's* a recommendation." He leaned forward, and Harriet was drawn into the swirling intensity of those deep, dark eyes. "I will pay you twice what those shares are worth just to have them in my control once more. My offer is more than fair."

Harriet rose abruptly. "I do not wish to have my shares in your control. I do not wish to have anything of mine in a man's control. I am my own mistress."

She turned away, but his hand caught her arm. "I see. Your much-vaunted independence is the real issue." His gaze narrowed. "Beware, madam. I will have them from you. You cannot best me at my own game. I have never met a woman who possessed the business sense of a man. You are no exception."

"And *you* are extraordinarily condescending," Harriet retorted. "How like a man to think that he knows best. You are no better than Squire Gibbs."

"There is no similarity between me and that idiot," he said indignantly.

"No?" she challenged. "Both of you want something from me. The only difference between you is that he has the effrontery to think he can win the mill by seduction. At least you do not have *that* shameful notion."

Harriet's face flamed as she heard her own words. But her heart positively rolled over in her breast at his reply.

"Do not be so sure."

As the stormy seas in his eyes gave way to something most unsettling, Lord Westwood pulled her close. One hand went around her waist, the other touched her chin and tilted it upward. Harriet caught her breath. Surely, he did not mean to—oh, dear, she thought, he did.

His lips brushed hers—once lightly, then again, more fleetingly. Harriet's pulse hammered wildly as his brief, vanishing kisses set off a tumult within her. She ought to have pushed him away—or boxed his ears. To her amazement, she merely closed her eyes and waited meekly for more.

But there was no more. Instead, he pulled away. Harriet's eyes flew open. Bemused, she stared at those sensual lips and wondered why they had abandoned her.

An inadvertent cry of disappointment emerged from deep in her throat. His lips quirked upward in amused satisfaction. Harriet flushed in anger and humiliation. This was precisely what he had intended—to demonstrate his masculine power by making her yearn for more.

Harriet detested men who tried to prove their mastery over women. How insulting that Lord Westwood thought she could be enslaved by such tiny, insignificant kisses. She would show him who was in charge.

Angrily, she gripped his arm.

His smile broadened. Undoubtedly, he thought that she meant to beg for another kiss, that his touch had actually affected her. He did not realize that no man moved her in that way. She would show him. She would give him a kiss to wipe all trace of amusement from his face. Then she would turn on her heel and leave him battling his desire.

Harriet parted her lips the way she was certain Lady Forth had done for Freddy so many times during their liaison. She pressed her mouth against his and felt his initial surprise give way to satisfaction as he returned her pressure in equal measure. His arms went around her waist. She nestled closer and felt his hands clench reflexively. She had him now. *He* would beg.

Harriet was not sure which of them deepened the kiss, but suddenly it erupted between them like a newborn volcano. The hot fires of an untried passion surged within her. And just like that she was hurled into turbulent seas, her ruthlessly calculating kiss dismissed by a tidal wave of sensation.

She had not foreseen that his seeking tongue would thrust into her mouth, filling her with its insistent and wholly masculine heat. Or that his searching hand would brush her breasts through the fabric of her gown, causing her insides to flutter like a butterfly. Or that his touch would ignite an unfamiliar warmth deep within her.

Most assuredly, she had not expected to find herself breathless and whimpering in an intimate iron embrace that eloquently revealed Lord Westwood's burgeoning enthusiasm for the exercise she had so boldly begun.

Freddy had never kissed her like this. He never seemed truly to desire her, and she had not known how to make him want her or how to give him pleasure. Their encounters in the marriage bed had been brief, impersonal, polite.

There was nothing polite in Lord Westwood's raw response. He nibbled her earlobe, where he found one excruciatingly sensitive spot that jolted her with pleasure, and trailed kisses down to the hollow of her throat. Every place his mouth touched turned white hot. Her nerves stood on end, tingling with anticipation and delight.

Harriet had not known that a kiss could leave one weak in the knees. No wonder her husband had developed a roving eye. She had failed to excite him. Poor Freddy! She had been a thoroughly inadequate wife.

That shocking realization ripped her from the immediacy of Lord Westwood's tantalizing kisses and flung her back to the difficulties of the past. Freddy had turned to other women because she was not woman enough. The repercussions of that bald revelation were almost unthinkable.

Lord Westwood lifted his head and regarded her from hooded eyes.

"Is something wrong?" he asked quietly.

Painful memories flooded back, along with the horrifying new knowledge that she had been responsible for Freddy's misery. She had driven him to his doom.

"Yes." Unexpected tears welled in her eyes. "I believe that I killed my husband."

Elias stood very still, getting himself under control, hoping that Lady Harriet would soon make some sense. He took a deep breath. His pulse was still galloping, his body still driven by the sexual urgings she had unleashed.

"According to the account provided to my solicitor," he said carefully, "Freddy's heart simply gave out. There is nothing you could have done one way or the other."

"I will never know, my lord. He was not at home that night." A tear ran down her cheek. "He was with another woman."

As Elias reached for his fresh handkerchief and handed it to her, part of his slowly awakening brain marveled at the speed with which she was disposing of the items in his traveling wardrobe. He was not entirely surprised to hear that Freddy had strayed. His partner had always had a weakness for women. A few words pronounced at a wedding ceremony would not have changed that.

"I am sorry," he said.

"I never cry," she said tremulously, wiping her eyes. Elias arched a brow. "I did not object to his liaisons," she continued after a moment. "Freddy deserved to be happy. I did not realize until now how much of his misery was my fault. I must have driven him to the life he led, to the very excesses that led to his death!"

"Nonsense." It irked him that the earth-rattling kiss they had shared triggered recollections of her faithless husband. "Freddy Worthington was incapable of fidelity."

She shook her head. "He would have been true to the right woman. He would not have spent his days wrecking his health with drink and other women had I been able to satisfy him."

"What do you mean?"

"You know." She made a gesture that encompassed the space between them—a space that had been no space at all a few moments ago. "Like . . . like *this*." Her watery blue eyes filled with embarrassment.

Elias cleared his throat. Damned if he would stand here discussing her intimate relations with Freddy. "Freddy had a defective heart. His death stemmed from no more and no less than that. It is useless to blame yourself and even sillier to wallow in self-pity."

Instantly, she brought her chin up. Her lips trembled, but she glared at him defiantly. Elias knew he had hurt her, but he could not allow her to blame herself for Freddy's death. If Freddy had not been satisfied in Lady Harriet's arms, it was the man's own damned fault.

She was meant for sensual delight—full, tempting lips, skin like creamy satin, breasts that demanded to be caressed and suckled. He had wanted to toss her onto the dining room table and get on with it.

"That was insensitive, my lord," she said coolly, fumbling to adjust the bodice he had so recently tried to plunder. "I suppose I should expect no less from a man bent on manipulating me."

Angrily, Elias closed the distance between them once more. "Foul, madam," he growled. "A minute ago, *you* were the manipulator. Do not deny that you relished pushing me to the edge, leaving me powerless."

"Powerless?" She stared at him. "Truly?"

With a low curse, Elias swept her into his arms. Before she could draw a breath, his lips claimed hers.

Now she would think no more of Freddy—only of him. He kissed her long and hard, breathing in her intoxicating scent. He caressed her breast and felt her heart thumping against him like the wings of a fluttering bird.

He kneaded the fabric of her skirt, bunching it up against her hips in his desperation to touch the smooth silk of her legs.

Elias had no idea what might have happened then in Lady Harriet's dining room, there amid the used coffee cups and plates filled with congealing eggs, if a shrill voice had not suddenly intruded.

"Harriet! Whoever is this man? And *what* is he doing to your, er, person?"

Chapter Four

"Poor Eustace!" Draping herself in one of the dining room chairs, Monica Tanksley took refuge in her smelling salts. "I cannot believe you have betrayed me like this, Harriet. Poor, *poor* Eustace!"

Harriet signaled to Horace to bring Monica sherry and the little iced cakes her neighbor loved. "Now, Monica, it is not what you think. Anyway, Eustace has no more regard for me than the man in the moon."

Monica gave her a reproachful gaze. "You do not know my son as I do," she said mournfully. "He is a dear, sensitive soul. To learn that you have given yourself to this . . . this *rakehell*, will be more than he could manage. He will be inconsolable."

Lord Westwood, who had remained silent throughout Monica's hysterics, was obviously offended by the unflattering characterization. Harriet took one look at his darkening features and decided that it would be prudent to take matters more firmly in hand.

"Monica, Lord Westwood is Freddy's former partner. He is here to consult with me on business matters. Nothing more." Although it was obvious that business had been far from their minds in the moment Monica discovered them.

Monica gave the earl a jaundiced eye.

"My pleasure, madam," Lord Westwood said curtly.

"Yes, I imagine it was," she retorted, arching a meaningful brow in Harriet's direction. Lord Westwood's scowl deepened.

In another moment they would be at fisticuffs. Harriet hastily grabbed the plate of cakes and made a great show of passing them around. As there was only Lord Westwood and Monica, this did not take very long. The earl gave Harriet a hard stare before condescending to take a piece of cake. He took a bite, shot her a surprised look, then took another. In the next instant, the entire piece had vanished.

"Exceptional," he said grudgingly, reaching for a second piece, which he devoured with equal speed.

" 'Tis the rose water that makes it special," Monica snapped.

"It is the mace," he corrected. "It marries well with the sugar but does not eclipse the underlayer of tartness that keeps the cake from being cloying."

"Lemon juice," Harriet put in helpfully. "Just a dash, mind you. It is one of my favor—"

"I still say it is the rose water," Monica groused, ignoring Harriet but regarding Lord Westwood with new interest.

"The hint of roses is all to the good," he conceded, "but you must own that the sweetness of the spice and sugar harmonizes perfectly with the citrus."

Monica stared at him with something approaching respect. "I have never met a man with such an understanding of food."

"Lord Westwood has a heightened sense of smell," Harriet offered. "Spices are his business. He searches the far seas for products that might appeal to our tastes, then arranges for them to be shipped here so that we can enliven our rather ordinary cuisine with a bit of the exotic."

The earl looked at her in surprise. "Never say that you actually have an inkling of what my business is about?"

"Of course," Harriet replied indignantly. "I hope you did not think me stupid."

"Anyone who sells off shares of a hugely profitable business for a fraction of their worth is a veritable peagoose," he said bluntly.

Harriet snatched the plate of cakes away just as he was about to snare a third piece.

The angry exchange was not lost on Monica. "Perhaps I misconstrued things," she conceded thoughtfully, studying them. "I expect it is only a fleeting attraction between you. I have heard that these things can happen." She paused, then added wistfully, "Not, unfortunately, to me."

"There is nothing between Lord Westwood and me," Harriet insisted. "We were only discussing the future of the business."

Monica merely shot her a knowing look and reached for another cake. Her hand stilled, however, at Lord Westwood's next words.

"To be quite truthful, Mrs. Tanksley," he said in a clipped voice, "she was trying to seduce me. I am pleased to say that I resisted. A gentleman has his reputation to think of. Good day, madam."

And with that, he strode from the room.

Harriet stared after him, overwhelmed both by fury and the urge to laugh. She felt Monica's gaze on her and managed a weak smile. "Lord Westwood is quite a wit," she said lamely.

Monica only shook her head in renewed dismay. "Oh, dear, Harriet. Oh, dear, dear, dear."

"I know what I saw, and it wasn't any business discussion." Heavenly eyed her sister meaningfully across the kitchen table. "He had his hands wandering all about."

"Right there over the coffee." Celestial sighed dreamily. "Such a forceful man, such robust appetites! That husband of hers never showed the least bit of interest in her before his port. More often than not he was too drunk to eat the special meals she prepared him, but Lord Westwood's plate comes back clean as a whistle."

"Lord Westwood has an appetite, all right, and not just for the eggs." Heavenly frowned. "He hasn't had his eyes off her since he came through the front door."

Horace tried to look stern, but in truth he was just as interested in what had transpired between his mistress and the earl. He had followed Mrs. Tanksley into the dining room in a vain attempt to announce her and had thus witnessed their shocking embrace. Heavenly had apparently been watching through the keyhole at the time.

"Lady Harriet would be distressed to know you had been spying," he said censoriously.

"Who is going to tell her?" Heavenly retorted. "Not I."

"Nor I," Celestial promised.

"If only you had seen her, Celestial." Heavenly shook her head in wonder. "Boldly kissing him like she knew what was what."

"He must have started it."

"Not a bit!" Heavenly insisted. "Oh, he gave her a little peck, but she's the one turned it into a thing to behold. I believe our lady is finally coming into her own." She grinned. "And not a moment too soon. After what that husband of hers put her through, she deserves to be happy."

Celestial nodded. "He was a scoundrel."

"You are speaking of our dear departed employer," Horace said reprovingly.

"There was nothing dear about him," Heavenly shot back.

Horace remained tactfully silent. He was not about to defend Lord Worthington, who had been, by anyone's reckoning, an utter cad. But he would not indulge in kitchen gossip, either. Or at least he would not appear to.

"It has been a year since the viscount's death," he said

in a neutral tone. "It is perfectly understandable that Lady Harriet wishes to enjoy a gentleman's company once more."

"No, it ain't," Heavenly corrected. "She is scared to death of men."

Horace frowned. "Not a bit. She runs the bakery, lives here alone, throws all those parties in town by herself. Why, Lady Harriet fears nothing."

Heavenly exchanged a meaningful look with her sister. "Men don't know anything, do they?"

Celestial gave a tsk-tsking sound and regarded Horace pityingly.

Slowly, it was beginning to dawn on Elias that he had compromised Lady Harriet. To be sure, no one had said anything about that. Her friend Mrs. Tanksley had been shocked at finding them together, but her dismay apparently stemmed from Lady Harriet's cavorting with someone other than her precious Eustace—though the lad sounded a bit young to take on a widow.

Cavorting. Was that what they had been doing? Cavorting sounded pleasant. Why had it left him feeling so dissatisfied and out of sorts and in need of delivering such an unpardonable parting shot—that obvious lie about Lady Harriet trying to seduce him?

To be sure, widows were not expected to comport themselves as virgins. But unless they wished to ruin their reputations, they did not allow men to make love to them in the dining room in easy view of any servant or friend who might drop by. And despite Lady Harriet's bold behavior, there was no denying that he had started things—and possibly would have finished them had not the interfering Mrs. Tanksley appeared.

Elias did not take transgressions lightly, especially his own. A man who compromised a woman was obliged to marry her. He did not want to marry Lady Harriet, although it would certainly make securing the shares easier. They would revert to him, and that would be the end of it. But marriage was a steep price to pay for regaining control of his business. Too steep. It would be one of the worst deals he had ever engineered.

He did not think Lady Harriet would wish to wed. Her insistence that she enjoyed being her own mistress made the prospect dubious. Unlike most women he had known, Lady Harriet seemed genuinely determined to steer her own boat.

Which would spell endless trouble for any man who married her.

No, he would not wed Lady Harriet. But he would do the honorable thing. He would offer for her, knowing that she would refuse. Thank God she was an independent sort.

The trouble with a small village is that the only people to entertain were those one saw every day. Harriet sighed as she put the finishing touches on her meal. She had invited the Tanksleys, Squire Gibbs, and Lord Westwood to dinner before the embarrassing events of yesterday had occurred. Now they would all sit around and shoot each other murderous looks. Her dinner would be a disaster.

Fortunately, she would soon remove to London, where her salons would be as lively and fascinating as ever, and where people knew how to comport themselves even when the discourse grew outlandish.

Every Season, Harriet removed to town—not for the parties and social whirl but for the stimulating talk that accompanied the arrival of Parliament. Over the years, her town house had become a noted gathering place for all manner of political figures from radicals to Tories. What flourished was a yeasty brew of ideas as scintillating as the sumptuous baked goods she served to accompany them. Her invitations were highly prized, though Freddy had preferred to spend his evenings elsewhere.

Last year she did not go to town. It had nothing to do with being in mourning. She had simply not wished to encounter Freddy's friends—especially Lady Forth, who knew all too well Harriet's failures as a wife.

Throughout her disastrous marriage, Harriet had kept an open mind, reasoning that Freddy had every right to seek his own happiness when he could not find it home. She did not regret her decision. But she did regret that all of London knew Freddy was sleeping with Caroline Forth. And Cecily Browning before that. And Lady Iris before that. And any number of flaming stars in the *ton*'s dazzling firmament. The only woman who no longer succumbed to his charms was his wife.

During her first and only London Season, Harriet had found Freddy a captivating diversion from the suffocating existence she led in her father's gloomy castle. She had been lonely and starved for affection, and Freddy had swept her away with his flattery and romantic ways. Harriet had wanted to love him, to share his bed, to find in another human being a warmth she had never known. After their wedding, she learned that she had mistaken his practiced charm for sentiment and that Freddy had fallen in love with her dowry, not the woman who possessed it. And though he granted her all the freedom a wife could want, he had no intention of compromising his own.

On the relatively rare times in which they engaged in marital intimacies, Harriet had felt nothing. After her initial disappointing discovery as to the true state of her marriage, she decided that things had worked out for the best after all. She did not try to cajole or wheedle or seduce her husband into her bed. Instead, she immersed herself in her salons and in various interests from politics to baking. They took up so much of her time that she almost forgot about Freddy's dalliances.

But every time she met Lady Forth at a party or the opera, she remembered. It had been there in the woman's pitying eyes, in the cool contempt with which she regarded Freddy's eccentric wife.

Harriet had never realized how inadequate a wife she had been until Lord Westwood had shown her how it was done, this thing between men and women. He drew out a side of her she had never known existed. She had never been bold before, never kissed any man on her own initiative—certainly not Freddy. When Lord Westwood had crushed her to him during those last heady moments in the dining room, Harriet realized how much she had yet to learn and how vulnerable she was in not knowing.

Along with that lowering truth came the surprising revelation that Lord Westwood would be an excellent teacher.

Just the knowledge that she had moved him to passion—had he actually said she left him powerless?—made her feel strong. For the first time since Freddy's death, she felt ready to go to London again, ready to face her husband's friends. Harriet wondered whether her new sense of power would vanish when Lord Westwood was no longer around.

At all events, it was time to leave the country. Squire Gibbs's behavior was becoming boorish. Monica's scheme to match her with Eustace was silly in the extreme. Harriet had grown so preoccupied she could not even think clearly. Why, she had even forgotten to bake that Egyptian sourdough for tonight.

"Do not forget to add the orange juice," she told Celestial. "Curry welcomes a bit of tang."

"Yes, Miss Harriet. Is that nice lord coming to dinner?"

Harriet nearly dropped the spoon she had just used to

sample the chicken curry. "Lord Westwood dines with us, Celestial. Why do you ask?"

Celestial shrugged. "No reason. He is a fine one to look at. No wonder you went around the bend a bit."

"Celestial!" Harriet made a small choking sound. "Never say you were spying on me!"

The cook gave a small guilty nod. "Don't worry, ma'am. None of us thinks any worse of you. If I had my way, I'd have a beau, too, but Heavenly won't hear of it."

Dear lord, her behavior was the talk of the household! "Heavenly?" Harriet managed. "What has she to say about the matter?"

Celestial put down her spoon. "Twins have a special bond, I guess. She doesn't want us to part. I keep telling her it wouldn't be like that, that we'd always be close, but she doesn't believe it. Every time I've thought of marrying, she's done something to ruin it."

"But you are a grown woman. You must be . . ." Harriet hesitated, uncertain. "About thirty?"

"Thirty-five," Celestial corrected. "Most women my age have birthed their children. Some even have grandchildren. I will never have a family if Heavenly has her way."

"You are old enough to make your own decisions."

Celestial shook her head. "Heavenly's always done things her way. There's not a man alive strong enough to change that. Funny, though, I thought you were the same way, ma'am, and now I see that I might have been wrong. So mayhap I'm wrong about Heavenly. We'll see."

Harriet regarded her intently. "Is there someone who has caught your fancy, Celestial?"

Celestial shook her head, but Harriet did not miss the shadow that crossed her features. "I do hope you are right about Heavenly," Harriet said gently, "but you are wrong about me. Lord Westwood means nothing to me."

"Mmm." Celestial gave her a speaking look. "That's

why you've been in here six times checking the curry, making sure I used only the special powder Lady Hester sent."

Harriet could not think of a suitable response.

"The monarchy is out of touch."

"Eustace!" his mother said reprovingly. "That is unacceptable talk."

"Come now, Monica," Lady Harriet interjected. "The country is rife with criticism of the Prince. Eustace says no more than what has already been said."

"Yes, Mother. There are many who think the current movement to reform Parliament must extend even further—to the royals themselves. Why do we need them? That fat Prince does nothing but squander our money—"

"Treason," pronounced Squire Gibbs in one of the few words he had uttered all evening. "Such talk is pure treason."

Mrs. Tanksley's gaze lingered on the squire. "I cannot think what has put such radical notions in Eustace's head," she said sorrowfully.

"Why, the state of the country, of course," said Lady Harriet. "The soldiers who fought so bravely abroad have found no jobs at home. Riots have erupted over the price of bread. Taxes have gone up, yet the Prince demands more and more money from Parliament to pay his debts."

Heaven spare him the company of a woman who dabbled in politics, Elias thought. Though he had no great love of the Prince, Elias had fought for the very government she scorned. He would never join the ranks of its public critics. He was determined, however, to keep these thoughts to himself, as his mind was occupied with more troubling ones. Such as how he was going to get her alone to make his obligatory marriage proposal.

Dinner had been excellent—he had come to expect no less—but afterward they had all engaged in stilted conversation in the drawing room. The convention of the gentlemen's port had been dispensed with, it being tacitly conceded that Squire Gibbs and he could have little wish to engage in polite discourse and that Eustace's presence was largely irrelevant.

It would soon be time for the guests to take their leave. Elias could think of no excuse to remain behind that would not risk branding Lady Harriet as his mistress and send Mrs. Tanksley into a deep decline over poor Eustace's depressed fortunes. Fortunately, help came from unexpected directions.

"My lord." Lady Harriet's soft, urgent tone intruded into his thoughts. "I must speak to you privately."

Cautiously, Elias surveyed the room. Squire Gibbs had grown morose and flushed from the wine. Mrs. Tanksley wore a disconcerted expression and was fanning herself rapidly. There seemed to be an awkward tension between the squire and Lady Harriet's friend—probably owing to Gibbs's denunciation of Eustace's views. Eustace himself looked thoroughly bored and not the least bit interested, incidentally, in pursuing a suit with Lady Harriet. When he saw Elias studying him, Eustace grinned and, with a conspiratorial air, rose and walked toward him.

"I can see you wish to get Lady Harriet alone," he whispered. "No one will think anything amiss if we all pretend to take a turn in the garden. Then I will leave you. This is no place for me."

Damned if he needed a half-fledged lad to tell him how to get a woman alone. But neither could Elias think of any other solution that would not send Mrs. Tanksley into hysteria and launch the squire into another of his tirades.

With an aplomb well beyond his years, Eustace made their excuses and accompanied Elias and Lady Harriet into the foyer. As he slipped furtively out the front door, Eustace winked broadly. Grimly, Elias eyed his surroundings.

The foyer opened into the parlor on one side, the dining room on the other, and was bisected by that flamboyant grand staircase. They might as well have been on stage, with eyes watching them from all corners. Elias was not about to make a marriage proposal, even a meaningless one, in a place where they could be disturbed at any time.

"Is there somewhere we can be private?"

Nodding, Lady Harriet led him to a small door that opened into a study. Hoping to prop up his sagging resolve, Elias regarded a plush leather chair longingly but decided that a proposal should not be made from the comfort of cowhide. Lady Harriet walked to a table that held a decanter and poured out two glasses. A wise move, he thought. Spirits would make this easier for both of them. He waited for her to bring him a glass.

Instead, she gulped down the entire contents of one glass and, after a deep breath, started on the other.

"May I, er, share some of that?" Elias asked politely.

A sudden sputtering told him that Lady Harriet was not as familiar with brandy as her actions indicated. "I am sorry, my lord," she said, coughing. "Where are my manners?" She poured out a third glass, which Elias gently took from her.

As he sipped his own brandy, Elias studied her. Thank God she had abandoned black bombazine tonight for something less off-putting. Her pale green dinner gown recalled the color of an exotic apple he had found growing incongruously on the northern coast of South America. Still, she looked excessively nervous, and he wondered what she wished to say to him. No matter—it would have to wait. He was determined to get this marriage proposal over with.

"Lady Harriet," he began in a formal tone. "I am sensible of the scandal I caused in your dining room yesterday. Your friend had every reason to assume the worst about your entertaining a man alone at that early hour of the morning. The manner in which we were discovered left little room for any other conclusion."

He thought he heard a small giggle. She covered her mouth and eyed him solemnly.

"It is not my wish to dishonor you, madam," he continued. "As a widow, you have your reputation to think of, and it is a gentleman's responsibility to think of it also. I regret that my actions compromised you. Therefore, I would like to rectify matters by offering marriage."

As marriage proposals went—and he had made only one previously, to disastrous effect—this was quite impersonal. He was certain that Lady Harriet would immediately recognize it for what it was, a sop to her reputation and nothing else. Though that embrace in the dining room had produced unexpected fireworks, there was no affection between them. Neither he nor Lady Harriet could possibly pretend otherwise.

Elias schooled his features to an expression of anxious waiting, when in truth he knew exactly what Lady Harriet would say: *"Thank you, my lord, but I must refuse. I am my own mistress. I do not wish to be under any man's control."*

He would allow his face to fall into an expression of deep regret. Then they would get on with the business of deciding the fate of her shares of Westwood Imports.

Lady Harriet leveled her clear blue gaze at him. "I accept."

Elias stood very still.

"I know it is not what you want," she added nervously. "Your proposal was tendered for reasons of honor. But I find that I need you just now. Indeed, sir, I was wondering how to muster the courage to propose to *you.*" At his shocked expression, she quickly added, "We need not really marry, of course, only pretend for a short while to be engaged."

"Pretend," he echoed, dazed.

She looked at him hopefully. "If you agree, I will give you my shares of your business."

It was what he wanted. And not.

Not, not, not.

Chapter Five

The brandy had made her slightly dizzy, but Harriet had no trouble discerning that she had stunned Lord Westwood beyond belief. He had not expected her to accept.

Part of her felt guilty for taking advantage of his code of honor, for there was really no need for him to have offered marriage. Monica was no gossip. She would not have spread the word about Harriet's indiscreet behavior.

Another part of her wished that her acceptance of his proposal had not caused him such obvious dismay. Did he loathe her so very much? Did another woman claim his affection? A man like Lord Westwood must have many female admirers.

"I am sorry. I know this has come as a shock." She lowered her gaze. "I should mention that I remove to London in a fortnight. I would expect you to do likewise—in the interest of recovering your shares, of course."

Lord Westwood drained the contents of his glass. "In the interest of recovering my shares," he said slowly, "I would do a great many things."

"Marrying me had not been at the top of your list though, had it, my lord? But you need only pretend to be my betrothed for a bit," Harriet assured him. "I will cry off by Season's end. If you wish, I will put that in writing."

He regarded her warily. "A sworn statement?"

"In the presence of our solicitors."

Lord Westwood squared his shoulders. "I have proposed marriage. You have accepted. I will honor whatever terms you set."

"In other words, you have no one to blame but yourself," Harriet said wryly.

He did not reply. The rueful look in his dark eyes was answer enough. For a brief moment, Harriet felt almost sorry for him. Then she pushed the thought away. By the end of their masquerade, he would be in full possession of his shares. It was a very good bargain for him.

"Why?" he asked simply.

Why indeed? It was difficult to explain. A man like Lord Westwood, who exuded confidence from every pore, would never understand.

"I have not been to town since Freddy's death," she began. Looking for courage, she took another sip of brandy. "I am my own person," she continued. "I do not need a man on my arm to make my day worthwhile, nor do I depend upon masculine appreciation for my own worth."

Lord Westwood ran a finger over the rim of his glass, but his gaze never left her face. His silence, and perhaps the brandy, made her rush to fill the gap. "My life is perfect," she added, a bit defensively. "I surround myself with good food and scintillating company. I intend to go on like this forever, happily enjoying my woman's independence. I do not need a man."

"So you have said."

Harriet flushed. "But I find that I do need you, at least for a few weeks. People will make a to-do over my return to town. I feel strangely reticent to face Freddy's friends, especially since I bear some blame for his death. I want to go on with my life, to learn from my mistakes. But I find that just now I need a . . . a suit of armor to help me face them." She eyed him apologetically. "That would be you, my lord. I hope you do not mind."

"Balderdash."

"I . . . what?" Harriet stammered.

His gaze narrowed. "You need no buffer against the world. Do not ask me to believe such poppycock."

Harriet looked away, uncertain as to how to respond to his challenge. "Perhaps I have not been completely frank," she conceded. "I have omitted something."

"And that would be . . . ?"

She took a deep breath. "The truth is, Lord Westwood, I would like to learn how to be a desirable woman."

The loud thump was the sound of his glass being deposited on the table. "Good God," he muttered.

"I told myself that it did not matter that Freddy did not want me." The words came out in a rush. "But it did matter. Because of me, he fell into unhealthful pursuits. In some way that I do not understand, I must do penance for that, my lord. I must learn how to be a proper woman, how to overcome my deficiency."

"Lady Harriet—"

"In the dining room yesterday, you said you were powerless." Harriet could not meet his gaze. "I am quite sure I never made Freddy feel powerless."

"There is no need to—"

"I do not have the slightest idea how to please a man, my lord," she continued, unable to stanch the humiliating flow of words. "In some way I do not understand, you help me overcome that. When I am around you, my lord, I feel stronger than I ever did with Freddy. And yet helpless at the same time. It is a strange feeling. I do not believe I have ever allowed myself to be helpless before. Perhaps that is where I have failed."

Harriet looked up at him. She had expected to see ridicule or even embarrassment in his eyes, but she was not prepared for the steely anger that glinted in that dark gaze. Lord Westwood's features hardened to granite, and he looked as if he did not trust himself to speak.

"And just how do you expect me to earn my shares?" he asked in a harsh voice.

Harriet eyed him blankly.

"A kiss . . . now that must be worth a dozen or so shares." His lips thinned disdainfully. "But at that rate it will take some time to win them all back. I will have to speed up the pace—a tumble on the seat of my carriage, for instance, might be worth as much as fifty shares."

Cocking his head, he stroked his chin as if pondering the matter. "Then again," he said in a musing tone, "I might be wrong. I have never put a price on my services. I thought only whores did that. Little did I realize I would some day become one."

Harriet paled. "You need only squire me around, spend time in my company in public. I do not expect you to make love to me, my lord. I never meant to suggest that."

"I see." He arched one brow. "You wish merely to learn how to feel desire—not to put it into practice."

"It will only be temporary," she assured him. "I would never wish to feel helpless for any length of time."

"Helpless." He shook his head in disbelief.

"My lord," Harriet prodded, "you will help me, will you not?"

"Do I have a choice, Lady Harriet?"

"One always has a choice, Lord Westwood."

"Until I met you, madam, I was foolish enough to think that was true."

"Yes or no, sir?" Harriet tapped her foot impatiently. She was tired and anxious—and beginning to think she had made an utter fool of herself.

He bent toward her. A dark, dangerous air suffused his gaze. "Oh, yes, my lady. I will dance to your tune, as it is the only one available at the moment. But I should not like to be in your shoes when the music changes."

* * *

In the end, she did sign a statement. Swearing on a Bible before Mr. Stevens, her astonished solicitor, on her very first day in town, Harriet promised to break her engagement to Lord Elias Westwood by August 12, the scheduled date for Parliament's adjournment. The papers were signed as their betrothal announcement was being prepared for the *Gazette*.

Then she returned to her town house and began to prepare a meal for fifty guests.

Removing to town had been surprisingly easy. Swamped by nervousness at the prospect of entertaining Lord Westwood alone in London for weeks, Harriet had prevailed upon Monica and Eustace to accompany her. Monica was delighted that Eustace would have an opportunity to acquire some town polish, though she heartily disapproved of Harriet's betrothal scheme and had not entirely given up on attaching Eustace to Harriet in the future.

"Eustace deserves a woman like you, Harriet," Monica had said as they drove away from Worthington. Eustace rode alongside the carriage. "You would be the making of him."

"He deserves a girl nearer his own age."

"He is eighteen. There is not six years between you."

"There is a lifetime between us, Monica. I have already buried one husband."

"He has no title, so it is not essential for him to marry a virgin," Monica replied frankly. "What I most want for him is a woman of worth. Like you, dear."

Harriet eyed her friend in amusement. "Nonsense. You only want me for a daughter-in-law so that you can be sure he is in good hands. You must cut the apron strings, Monica. Eustace must find his own future, not fall into the one you have fashioned for him."

"I suppose you are right," Monica said dejectedly.

"The heart ever goes where it will. I learned that when Francis ran off with my maid. Curse his lecherous soul. How fitting that he died on that ship to the colonies. A cold, watery grave suits him."

"What Francis did was regrettable, but it was long ago. You must bury the past. Perhaps in London you will meet someone who takes your fancy."

"I would rather see how Lord Westwood takes yours."

Harriet frowned. "I do not know what you mean."

"Do you not?" Monica sighed. "My dear, I fear you are headed for disaster. This masquerade is the most ridiculous and dangerous notion you have ever devised."

"Not at all. It provides Lord Westwood a way to recover his shares. And I will learn what I did wrong with Freddy."

"So that you can be a better wife for the next man, I suppose."

Harriet shook her head. "There will be no next man. I shall not wed again. But I can better my understanding of relations between the sexes. Lord Westwood strikes me as an adequate teacher, despite having the disposition of a bear."

"An adequate teacher? Oh, I suspect so." Monica eyed her pityingly. "You are a lamb, Harriet."

"Lamb?" Harriet laughed. "I have been a married woman, remember?"

"Marriage to Freddy cannot have prepared you for this game with a man like Lord Westwood," Monica warned.

"It is not a game," Harriet retorted. "It is a business arrangement."

"Business. Of course."

Monica was the only one she had told of the fraudulent nature of her betrothal. Heavenly and Celestial had accepted the news of her betrothal with surprise and glee, and even Horace had unbent sufficiently to allow himself a broad grin of congratulations.

The ladies at the bakery were also overjoyed and promised to look after things in her absence, as they had always done. On her last day in Worthington, Harriet had even taken Lord Westwood around to meet them. They loaded him down with a basket of her petit pastries and all manner of delicacies to take on his trip, for he was journeying to London ahead of them. But when he searched in his pockets for payment, Harriet put a hand on his arm.

"Oh, you must not," Harriet had admonished.

"But I cannot accept such a gift," he protested.

"You must. We do not accept money here."

He frowned. "Ever?"

"The bakery is for the benefit of all."

"You give away your goods?" He eyed her incredulously. "The shop's losses must be astonishing. Why, the price of bread alone is substantial."

Harriet nodded. "Exactly. It is so high that no one can afford it. We give it away to all who need it. In exchange, they put in a few hours each week making more bread. That way, the bakery largely pays for itself. It is the same with the mill. People who grow wheat may use the mill without cost as long as they donate a portion of the flour to the bakery. The system works quite well. I have heard no complaints other than from Squire Gibbs, and only because his income has been greatly reduced. I have a job for him, if he would but listen to me. But his pride has prevented him from doing so."

"You would employ the man who assaulted you?" Lord Westwood had sounded appalled.

"Sometimes one's dearest friends come from the ranks of former enemies—do you not think so, my lord?"

"What I think is that you live in a world of fairy tales." With those parting words, Lord Westwood had tucked the basket under his arm and departed for town.

Now Harriet stood in her own kitchen in London, staring at the bowl of almonds Celestial had assembled for grinding. Harriet insisted on making the almond cheesecakes herself for this, her first party in town. She never knew exactly how much orange-flower water to add, but it was always just right. Celestial's feel for pastries was less sure, though her intricately mixed herbal preparations revealed the instincts of a culinary artist.

Lord Westwood was mistaken. She did not live in a world of fairy tales. Her feet were firmly grounded in reality. Harriet knew exactly what she was doing. A woman on her own must be prepared. A wealthy widow would be fair game to seducers and fortune hunters—Squire Gibbs had shown her that. Harriet had always been protected, first by her father, then by the niche she had carved out for herself as Freddy's wife. She had thought herself able to manage any man, but Lord Westwood had shown her that she was not so strong as she thought. Indeed, she had almost succumbed to him in her very own dining room.

That was the root of the secret she had told no one—not Monica, certainly not Lord Westwood. She meant to uncover the mystery of his magic, so that she would know it for so much smoke and mirrors.

Knowing the reason for her weakness to Lord Westwood would enable her to resist, to escape heart-whole from the terrifying undercurrents of a world ruled by men.

And then she would never, ever, be hurt by a man again.

Chapter Six

"I've seen you face combat in a happier state."

"Thank you, Henry. As always, your views are inescapable." Elias glowered at his batman. The news of his betrothal had left Henry uncharacteristically silent for a full thirty seconds, but he had quickly recovered to state his opinion in blunt terms.

Elias saw no need to disclose the exact nature of the betrothal. More than once he wished for someone to tell him that he had not lost his mind in agreeing to Lady Harriet's outlandish plan, but Henry would not have been the one to turn to. At forty, he was a decade older than Elias and even more confirmed in his bachelorhood. And while Elias had once come close to marriage, Henry had never been tempted by the institution and thought it a disastrous state in general. Indeed, Henry had barely contained his relief when the Honorable Miss Zephyr Payne left Elias standing at the altar, a white rose in his lapel and humiliation on his face.

Not that Henry wished him unhappiness. The batman was as loyal and devoted as the day was long. But his loyalty had always been applied to comrades in arms—never to females. Females were a necessary evil, but that was not to say they belonged permanently in a man's life.

Come to think of it, that summed up his own philosophy these days. Why, then, had he entered into a betrothal, even a fraudulent one? Oh, yes—his shares, his precious shares, without which he could not rest easy at night, knowing that Lady Harriet was dedicated to throwing their worth away on every useless cause she could find.

That was the sole reason he had embarked on this mad masquerade. It had nothing to do with how she gazed up at him from eyes as blue as the sea on a cloudless day. Or how those errant auburn curls looked dusted with flour. Or how she felt in his arms, all wanton and wild and willing.

Elias stared at his scowling reflection in the mirror. Lines of disapproval bisected his forehead just above his nose. His jaw tensed forbiddingly. Henry was right. He looked as if he were headed for his doom.

"Do not wait up," he barked. "I do not know when I will return." Because he had no idea what Lady Harriet expected of him on this, the first night after the *Gazette* officially proclaimed them betrothed. Did she wish him to stay by her side like a fawning supplicant, to linger adoringly after the guests had departed?

The role of paid paramour did not suit him. He would rather take on Napoleon and all his eagles than face this one eccentric widow tonight. As his coachman maneuvered through packed streets to Berkeley Square, Elias's mood grew darker and darker. He had thought himself so clever. He had been certain he could bend her to his will and regain his shares, one way or another.

Instead, he had lost his head and unwisely made love to her in her dining room over breakfast. Now he was about to be paraded before her friends like a circus animal so that she could improve her knowledge on the subject of desire.

Elias did not like being bested in any endeavor. Most especially, he did not like being bested by a woman. If she wished to learn about desire, she would get more than she bargained for.

For the first time since arriving in London, Elias felt the beginnings of a smile.

"Corruption. All around. In this very room, if I may be frank." With a smile, Oliver Hunt met Harriet's gaze, then turned to those gathered around him. "Beware the rich aristocrats in Parliament who profess to be in sympathy with the plight of the downtrodden."

As many of those same aristocrats were standing in Harriet's parlor, a few nervous titters echoed around the room. Harriet frowned. She did not mind Mr. Hunt's radical oratory; her parlor had seen more than its share over the years. What disturbed her was the portentous smile he had bestowed upon her all evening. And though he had offered felicitations over her betrothal, he had eyed Lord Westwood with ill-concealed disdain.

Mr. Hunt's visage was normally stern, as befit a revolutionary. He was a man with a cause, and his cause—just or no—consumed him. He ought not to be smiling at his hostess as if they shared something special. Harriet had seen him a time or two since Freddy's death. Once he had even come to visit her in Sussex on his way to a political gathering. But there had been nothing between them, nothing to generate that riveting warmth in his eyes. She was not attracted to him, although Mr. Hunt possessed a compelling presence. As he spoke, he made eye contact with every member of his audience and, like all skilled orators, used his smooth, rumbling baritone to mesmerizing effect.

"What is the cause of the want of employment?" he demanded, lifting his voice to the arched ceiling as if it were the vaulted dome of some majestic cathedral. "What is the reason our streets are filled with idle, able-bodied men?" He paused dramatically, then raised his finger heavenward. "Taxation! Taxation is the cause of the country's decay."

A lock of fiery red hair tumbled over his high forehead. A bit younger than Lord Westwood, Mr. Hunt exuded an energetic fervor that made him appeal to young men like Eustace, who had been eyeing him worshipfully all evening. Yet he commanded the attention of older men as well. The audience included Tories and Whigs alike, along with some of the leading opinion writers of the day. Though most were accustomed to inflammatory rhetoric and absorbed his words dispassionately, Eustace seemed truly affected.

As did Lord Westwood. But while Eustace regarded Mr. Hunt with open adoration, the earl could barely contain his irritation. Harriet guessed he had little use for men of words. Indeed, he seemed to have little use for any of her guests. All evening he had held himself to a standard of civility that failed to mask his chilly displeasure at being forced to do so. Her betrothal had caused quite a stir, and everyone was eager to meet him. But he had refused to play the enchanted fiancé and had accepted the many congratulations with grim resignation.

Harriet had already tried to placate him with several almond cheesecakes. Though he had pronounced them excellent, they had not altered his mood. And so, instead of mingling with her guests, nurturing the seeds of conversation and keeping the mix of ideas brewing, Harriet had felt obliged to keep a watchful eye on Lord Westwood. She hoped his forbidding countenance did not presage something disastrous that would ruin her party. By his own admission, he had a temper. She did not know him well enough to judge how long that civil veneer would hold.

At the moment, it looked thin indeed.

"And what is the cause of taxation?" Mr. Hunt continued, his voice rich with passion. "Corruption. The same corruption that enabled our leaders to wage that bloody war against Napoleon, which had for its object the destruction of liberties of all countries, but principally of our own."

Suddenly, the coiled tension in the man beside her unleashed. Harriet felt Lord Westwood gather himself, as if for battle.

"If Napoleon had ridden up to Whitehall," Lord Westwood said in an icy tone that knifed through the room, "doubtless you would have held his horse so that he could dismount."

Mr. Hunt's startled gaze flew to the earl, and a sense of foreboding seized Harriet. The man's oratory skills were such that only the intrepid dared to challenge him. Even as she watched, a slow smile spread over his features. It was the smile of a man who has spied an easy prey. He nodded in Lord Westwood's direction.

"A former military man," he said in a knowing tone, winking at the audience. "They always take offense when I challenge the cause that sent them into the devil's arms. One would think they welcomed death and destruction. Perhaps they are all barbarians at heart."

Lord Westwood leveled an unflinching gaze at his attacker. "And perhaps," he said quietly, "they merely wished to save England."

"Hear, hear!" came the approving cries. People moved closer, sensing a rousing debate.

"Save England?" Mr. Hunt regarded him in mock surprise. "Why, I wonder? So that the royalty can fatten itself on the backs of the people? Some victory, my friend. Did you know that the Prince has just asked for another fifty thousand pounds to pay his debts? That Parliament, in its infinite wisdom has just expanded the Princess Charlotte's allowance to sixty thousand pounds to support her own splendor and that of her husband? And that if the Prince of Coburg survives his amiable consort, he may draw from our taxes fifty thousand pounds a year?"

Lord Westwood remained silent. Mr. Hunt's lips curled

cynically. "Tell me, Westwood: Are we to have the pleasure of forever footing the royals' outlandish bills?"

People shifted nervously. Though harsh, Mr. Hunt's accusations were nothing more than truth. Even the most conservative among them thought the Prince's debts excessive. Harriet wondered how Lord Westwood, a man who kept his own words to a minimum, could hope to best Mr. Hunt's oratory.

"We did not fight for the royals," Lord Westwood replied calmly. "We fought so that our mothers and fathers and children could retain their freedom."

"Freedom?" Mr. Hunt scoffed. "The freedom to subject ourselves to forced taxation, you mean."

"No. The freedom that allows you to stand here tonight and spout such nonsense without having your head removed from your shoulders for treason."

The room erupted in laughter. Someone applauded. The tension immediately dissipated as the audience regarded Lord Westwood approvingly. Harriet sighed in relief and eyed the earl in reluctant admiration.

Mr. Hunt looked decidedly nonplussed.

"It seems that Lady Harriet's betrothed disagrees with me." His mouth pulled into an expression of mock dismay as he tried to salvage his position. "I hope that does not mean that my presence here will be unwelcome in the future." He shot Harriet an ingratiating smile.

Harriet opened her mouth to assure him that it did not, but Lord Westwood spoke first. "Lady Harriet's friendships will always receive my undivided attention," he said quietly.

It was an inescapable warning. Anger suffused Hunt's features, but he evidently decided to cut his losses. Without another word, he turned to address some of his youthful admirers. For the moment, at least, a crisis had been averted. But unsettling undercurrents lurked between the two men—and between her and Lord Westwood.

By the time her guests took their leave, Harriet was more than ready to be alone. Her head throbbed from the tension of the night. Her feet ached from standing sentry at Lord Westwood's side all evening, wondering whether he would do something untoward.

"You can relax now."

Harriet jumped. He had barely spoken since the exchange with Mr. Hunt, and now he stood next to her, watching the last of her guests depart.

"I am perfectly relaxed," she insisted. "I enjoy these evenings immensely."

"That is why your head aches like the devil."

Harriet closed her eyes, unable to deny the obvious. She put her fingers to her temples and massaged them.

"Did I disappoint, madam? Perhaps I should have upended the furniture or smashed Mr. Hunt's overactive jaw. You seemed to expect no less." His sardonic tone added to the painful drumbeat in her head. "But despite what your Mr. Hunt insinuates, I am not a barbarian."

Harriet flushed. "I never thought so, my lord."

"No?" He eyed her scornfully. "How else do you regard a man you hired to try to seduce you?"

She gasped. "I never—"

"Not expressly. But that is what you wish, is it not? You want to be tested. You wish to learn why it is that my kisses moved you and Freddy's did not. And then you wish to throw them all back in my face as I grovel for those shares of mine as payment. I will tell you one thing, madam: If Freddy were here tonight, I would thrash him for turning you into such a manipulative shrew."

"Shrew!" It was too much. All of the strains of the evening were contained in her outraged cry. "How dare you?"

Harriet launched herself at him, pummeling his chest with her gloved fists. "You know nothing about Freddy and me! You are just a . . ."

"Barbarian?" he suggested softly, capturing her wrists and thus rendering her blows utterly ineffective.

Fury and frustration warred within her. Frustration won the day. Tears welled in her eyes. "This is dreadful. I am never overset . . . never! It is so lowering."

But he was not listening. Even as he held her in his iron grip, even as her tears fell onto his lapel, an intrigued look swept his features.

"What is that scent?" he asked. "Not lavender, surely, nor orange blossoms, but something sweet." Abruptly, he buried his nose in her hair, inhaled deeply, then regarded her pensively. "Almost like . . ."

"P-p-primrose," Harriet stammered. "I mix it with a few crushed wildflowers. Otherwise, I would smell of the kitchen."

"Instead, you smell of the flowers that grow by the side of the road, wild and free, daring anyone to pick them." Lord Westwood regarded her with a curious expression. The forbidding lines in his face had vanished.

Stunned, Harriet could only stare at him. That, as it turned out, was a mistake. Swirling, enigmatic currents filled his dark eyes, drawing her into those dangerous depths. Harriet felt strangely weak. She swallowed hard, suddenly aware that they were very alone in the foyer.

Cautiously, she withdrew her hands from his grip. He did not object, but let her wrists slide slowly over his fingers. Stepping quickly out of his reach, Harriet tried to recover her poise.

"I apologize for my outburst, my lord. I am not ordinarily aroused to such passions."

"Perhaps that is your difficulty."

"Difficulty?" she echoed. "I have no difficulty." He arched a brow, as if to suggest he possessed some special knowledge that had eluded her. Irritation surged within her. "Incidentally, Lord Westwood," Harriet added, bristling, "I did *not* hire you to seduce me."

"No?" A gleam of amusement leapt to his gaze.

"Certainly not," she retorted.

"Does that mean I should not try?"

"Try?"

"To seduce you."

For the first time, Harriet began to suspect that she had made a very bad bargain in her arrangement with Lord Westwood. "No, my lord, you should not," she said, trying to keep her voice calm. "You should make yourself amiable and not insult my friends and endeavor to spend some time in the same room with me without looking as though it is the worst sort of torment."

"Very well."

Before she could reply, his lips brushed hers—just the slightest touch for the merest of moments, the space of time it took her to inhale. Her body startled into shameless pleasure at the sudden contact.

And then he was gone—out the door, into the night.

Harriet took a deep, uneven breath. The air flowed into her lungs, easing some of the strain. But the tension remained, wrapped around her insides like a vise.

"Spying again?"

Celestial jumped back from the dining room door. Horace stood there regarding her contemptuously. "I heard Lady Harriet crying, and I thought she might need assistance," she explained lamely.

"And did she?"

"I-I'm not sure. She seemed upset. Perhaps I ought to take her a sleeping potion. I just mixed a new batch of valerian."

Horace eyed her skeptically. "Lady Harriet is never upset."

"That is why I thought she needed help," she retorted.

Horace's face darkened in anger. "Lady Harriet's discussions with Lord Westwood are none of our concern. If I catch you spying on them again, I will—"

"You'll what?" Celestial demanded. "Admit it, Horace. You're just as curious as Heavenly and me about what's going on. I've seen you study the two of them when you didn't think anyone was looking."

He reddened. "I wish for Lady Harriet's happiness. I only wonder whether the earl can give it to her."

"Since when have you become an expert on what makes a woman happy?" Celestial challenged.

Abruptly, the fire left his features. "I—" Horace broke off, then looked at her helplessly. His face had gone suddenly pale. Whatever he wished to say was apparently beyond him. He turned and fled through the door.

Alone in the darkened dining room, Celestial stared after him and emitted a long-suffering sigh.

Chapter Seven

"So you see, Stevens, I have enough evidence to warrant a thorough investigation." Elias towered over the solicitor in whose presence two days ago he had watched Lady Harriet sign her pledge to terminate their betrothal by the Season's end.

Winston Stevens removed his spectacles and cleaned them carefully and deliberately, so as not to appear alarmed. But Elias had seen trapped men before, and this one bore all the signs. His pupils were dilated, and a thin film of sweat covered his brow. His hands trembled ever so slightly as he rubbed the lenses, buying time.

As well he might. Westwood Imports was extremely valuable. For years Elias's friends and associates had besieged him to sell them stock, but he preferred to keep the business in his control. Only he and Freddy, who had provided much of the company's initial investment, held shares. The shares Stevens had sold for Lady Harriet would have been snapped up, and at a hefty price. The mill repairs, sheep, cows, and other improvements she had made amounted to only a few thousand pounds. Stevens must have pocketed the rest.

"Since I have made you a rich man, however inadvertently, it seems only fitting that I be the one to remedy that fact," Elias continued.

Stevens put his spectacles on his nose. "You have no proof."

"Proof," Elias echoed in a musing tone. "Perhaps you are right. I could go to the trouble of getting an accounting from Lady Harriet as to the precise sums she received from you."

He walked around the edge of the man's desk. "And since I have a very good idea who in London would have leapt at the chance to buy into Westwood Imports, it would be a simple matter to track down the purchasers—who would be only too happy to produce the bills of sale. Any discrepancy between the sums Lady Harriet received and the purchase price will produce a trail that leads directly to you, Stevens. The proof, you see, can be had."

Stevens was no idiot. He knew when he was beaten. A sickly pallor swept his features.

"I did not mean to hurt Lady Harriet," he began, mopping his brow with his handkerchief. The little weasel looked ready to crawl under the desk.

"Lady Harriet will not press charges—providing you cooperate." Elias neglected to mention that his betrothed had no idea he had discovered Stevens's nefarious scheme.

Stevens sighed in relief, but a wary look crept into his eyes. "Cooperate? Then you will want restitution? Unfortunately, my lord, the money has already been spent. I had a large number of expenses. Debts, that is." He shot Elias an apologetic smile.

"Perhaps I neglected to mention that Miss Marigold Bennett is prepared to give evidence as to the nature of those expenses. I imagine your wife will be very interested to hear her testimony—not to mention your other clients, who may find that they, too, have funds due them."

"Marigold? Oh, no, my lord, you cannot!" Stevens slumped over the top of his desk.

Watching a man's disintegration was not pleasant, but

Winston Stevens more than deserved his fate. According to Elias's solicitor, Jeremy Wilson, Stevens had often bragged to colleagues about his talented mistress. It had been reasonable to assume that he had also bragged to his mistress about his embezzlement schemes. When Miss Bennett had met them at Wilson's office this morning, she confirmed his theory—and pocketed a hundred pounds for her trouble.

"Enough," Elias commanded coldly. Stevens did not deserve his pity. Greed had brought about the man's ruin. "The only way to avoid prison is to make restitution."

"B-b-but I have no money," Stevens stammered.

"There are other means by which you can make amends."

"Anything!" Stevens said fervently. "My lord, you have no idea how I regret my actions."

Elias rolled his eyes. The man was coming it a bit too brown, but at least he was willing. "I will require a complete list of the purchasers and the precise number of shares sold to each. I will also require an accounting of how many shares Lady Harriet still owns."

Stevens nodded eagerly. "Yes. I have that information." He raced to a file drawer, pulled out a sheaf of papers, and thrust them into Elias's hands.

Elias perused the documents. Many of the names were familiar to him. Some were not, but his solicitor would track them down. Unlike Winston Stevens, Jeremy Wilson was a diligent, dedicated, and honest man.

There was one surprise on the list. "Oliver Hunt?" Elias scowled, the memory of last night's encounter with the demagogue still fresh. "I thought his interest was in politics, not business."

"He approached me with an offer—last fall, I think—apparently at Lady Harriet's suggestion." Stevens gave him an ingratiating smile. "Perhaps Mr. Hunt is hedging his bets against the vagaries of a political career."

Hedging his bets? Yes, that was possible. But not against the failure of his politics. Hunt was so convinced of his own brilliance that he would never consider the possibility of failure. No, if Hunt was hedging his bets, it had something to do with Lady Harriet.

Elias tucked the list into his pocket. The information about Hunt was vaguely disquieting, but what Stevens's files revealed was more so. Lady Harriet had sold off nearly half of Freddy's shares, more than Elias had expected. It would cost a pretty penny to buy them back, and he would still have to regain her remaining shares.

There were encouraging signs, however. The lady had lost her composure last night, something she declared highly unusual. In his experience, when ladies lost their composure, it invariably meant that victory was near.

As he strode out of Winston Stevens's office, Elias banished the stench of the man's dishonesty with comforting thoughts of primroses.

"I have been wanting to try spelt for ages." Harriet regarded the lump of dough resting comfortably in a large bowl.

"Eustace did not come home until dawn," Monica said glumly.

"The dough is soft, almost satiny, and requires little kneading," Harriet marveled, oblivious to her friend's worried features.

"London is ruining him. He looks like a Cossack with those voluminous trousers and high collars. I do not see how he can manage to turn his head."

"Did you know that spelt has been used for thousands of years? I have Lady Hester to thank for this shipment."

"He has no money to gamble, so he must have spent his time with a woman. Of the worst sort, no doubt. *A woman!* My poor Eustace!" Monica began to weep. "If only you had taken him under your wing."

Startled, Harriet looked up from her worktable. "Oh, dear, I am afraid I have not been attending. You are worried about Eustace?"

Monica blew her nose. "Harriet, sometimes it is maddening to have you as a friend."

"I am sorry." Harriet wiped her hands on a towel and moved to embrace her. She eyed Monica affectionately. "Now, what is this new catastrophe?"

"Eustace did not come home last night. He rolled in just as the servants were stirring this morning, still in his evening clothes."

"Surely, it would have been worse had he *not* been in them," Harriet offered gravely.

Monica sniffed. "He does not know how to conduct himself among these sophisticated people. It was a mistake for us to have come to London. He is being exposed to all manner of creatures, like that odious Mr. Hunt."

"Oliver Hunt?" Harriet looked surprised. "He may be a rabble-rouser, Monica, but he is harmless."

"Harmless? What do you know, Harriet? You think it delightful to have all of these strange people in your parlor, fomenting rebellion—"

"Mr. Hunt was not fomenting rebellion," Harriet interjected. "The man likes to practice his rhetoric, but I do not think four out of five people hold with his views."

Monica rose. "Ah, but the *one*! The one in five caught by Mr. Hunt's seductive aura . . . that is Eustace!"

Harriet covered the dough with a towel. "He did seem rather enthralled last night, but he is of an age when new ideas and new people catch his fancy."

Monica shook her head in disgust. "Sometimes you have your head in the clouds. You blind yourself to the truth. It was the same with Freddy, and now, Lord Westwood."

"Freddy?" Harriet frowned. "Whatever do you mean?"

"The way you turned a blind eye to his philandering. I hated to see you so degraded."

Harriet paled. "It was not degrading. And my eyes were wide open. Do not condemn my behavior because you do not understand it."

"You tolerated his womanizing. What is there to understand?"

"That I am not wedded to anyone else's notions of what my behavior should be. That I did not wish to stifle Freddy's happiness. His activities did not hurt me in the slightest. Marriage should not be an institution that stifles the unique natures of both parties."

"I see. Then may I assume you had affairs as well?"

"Certainly not," Harriet said indignantly.

"So it was only Freddy's unique nature that required unstifling?"

Harriet stared at her friend. "Why are you doing this, Monica?"

"Because I want you to see that you walk through the world with blinders on when it comes to men. Because I want you to realize that not every man has your best interests in mind when he whispers pretty words in your ear."

"Lord Westwood did *not* whisper pretty words in my ear," Harriet said firmly.

Monica blinked. "I thought we were discussing Freddy."

"Actually, we were discussing Eustace," Harriet said quickly. "What does any of this have to do with him?"

"Eustace is an innocent, just like you—and for all that you have been married, Harriet, you are still a babe in the woods. He will be victimized, just as you were victimized. I live in terror that my only son will have his heart broken—just as you did."

Harriet stood very still. "Monica Tanksley, I have never had my heart broken. And I never will."

Monica regarded her for a long moment. Then she sighed. "Very well. Tell me more about this . . . spelt, is it?"

For the first time since being caught in Lady Harriet's unsettling orbit, Elias regarded the whirl of activity around him with the knowledge that it was comfortingly normal.

Lady Symington's ball was just like every other London ball during the height of the Season. The hostess and her husband greeted an interminable line of guests as an orchestra tuned its instruments and a flurry of servants prepared for the late-night supper that would send them all home stuffed and satiated until they could rise at midday and prepare to do it all over again.

Thank God that sort of life was behind him. He had almost gotten sucked into it permanently, when Zephyr Payne had accepted his marriage proposal. The daughter of Lord Ellwood Payne, one of Lord Castlereagh's intimates, Zephyr had been tending the wounded at the London hospital where Elias was recovering after being invalided home. In his weakened state he had taken one look at her delicate, heart-shaped face and sparkling green eyes and been lost.

How silly the notion seemed now. If he had married Zephyr, he would not have been free to roam the world in search of delectable spices with which to build his fortune. He would be shackled to a wife and children, reduced to dressing up like a penguin every night and attending boring events like this one. He should be eternally grateful that Zephyr had chosen not to present herself that morning at St. George's, Hanover Square, and elected to run off with Lord Pembroke instead.

He had not felt especially grateful, however. Even now, when he thanked his stars that his life was very different from the stifling fate that had awaited him with Zephyr, his veins still surged with anger.

The entire *ton* had assembled to witness the union of Lord Payne's beautiful daughter and the dashing earl wounded on the Peninsula in the heroic service of his country. It had required all of Elias's military discipline to stand for three-quarters of an hour in front of staring, whispering guests who wondered why Lord Westwood's bride had chosen to be late to her own wedding. The music went on interminably as the orchestra worked to fill the time.

At last a red-faced Lord Payne had drawn him aside, clutching a missive from his errant daughter explaining that she was likely enjoying Lord Pembroke's husbandly embrace by now. Elias had bowed stiffly and, without a backward look, walked calmly out into the blazing sunshine.

Humiliation did not set well with him, and having his suit repudiated in such a public fashion before the cream of society was humiliating in the extreme. Oddly, he had not vented his rage. He had simply gone on, with cool resolve, to make another life. But he had not forgotten that day. He had not entered a church since. And he had never allowed himself to form another serious liaison.

Elias's gaze narrowed as he watched Lady Harriet leave the dance floor with one of her many admirers. Her salmon-colored gown made him think of that first delicious meal she had prepared for him. Indeed, she looked good enough to eat tonight. He wondered whether the men who surrounded her thought so. They were not the usual dandies and tulips who cared more for the state of their leg padding than a lady's comfort. Lord Castlereagh had danced with her, and Lord Holland, too. Sir Thomas Lawrence had sought her out. Her current partner was an older man who looked as out of place among the glitter as a humble pigeon at Michaelmas. He was holding forth on some topic with great energy, and Lady Harriet was listening intently and with obvious respect.

None of her partners were the sort to rouse in him the least bit of jealousy, though if Lady Harriet had truly been his betrothed, her popularity might have given him pause. For even a man so advanced in years as the earnest gentleman she was presently entertaining might harbor designs on so lovely a woman.

Elias reminded himself that Lady Harriet was not his type. The sort of female who appealed to him did not send his pulse galloping wildly each time she entered the room. The excitement he preferred could easily be satiated; it did not last long, nor keep him up at night wondering whether he had done something foolish by kissing her.

The women he enjoyed did not deny their desire. They did not flail at him wildly and then disavow any acquaintance with passion. Most certainly, they did not dump foul-smelling goo on his head or force him to barter his person in exchange for the shares of his own business.

The sort of female who appealed to him understood the nature of lust and did not view it as anything more complicated. Rather like the woman who now stood at his elbow, as a matter of fact, regarding him with exotic, deep-set eyes.

"Good evening, Lord Westwood." She did not lower her lashes or flutter them in a silly fashion. She did not show him a virgin's pretty blushes. She looked straight at him, her velvet brown gaze meeting his without betraying a hint of coarseness even as they sparkled with invitation.

Elias bowed. A portrait of sophistication in a lemon yellow gown with daring but not scandalous décolletage, the woman had piled her glossy chestnut hair high on her head, leaving one tantalizing tendril free to grace her bare shoulder. "You have the advantage of me, madam."

"I am Lady Caroline Forth, a friend of your late associate, Lord Worthington." Though there was nothing coy in her manner, Elias's instincts immediately told him that this delectable creature had been Freddy's mistress.

"It is a pleasure to meet you, Lady Forth."

She inclined her head, accepting the compliment as her due. "I was surprised to learn that Lady Harriet planned to remarry," she said easily. "She seems so much more comfortable on her own. You must have charmed her, my lord. I imagine you are very good at it."

Her eyes were wide with innocence, but a clear invitation lurked within them.

Yes, this was just the sort of female he preferred—one who would not excite him to rage or rashness, but to simple, uncomplicated lust.

Chapter Eight

Harriet greatly respected William Wilberforce. A tireless advocate of reform, he had helped win passage of the bill abolishing the slave trade. Since he did not care for social gatherings, she had been surprised and delighted to find him at Lady Symington's ball. He ought to have had her undivided attention. Instead, it was riveted on two figures across the room: Lord Westwood and Lady Forth.

"The bill was a step," Mr. Wilberforce was saying, "but I will not rest until slavery itself is abolished—"

"Nor should you," Harriet agreed, her gaze straying over Mr. Wilberforce's shoulder to lock with Lord Westwood's half a room away. Her fiancé nodded absently at her, then returned his attention to the ravishing Caroline.

"Nor should we *all*," Mr. Wilberforce corrected. "Anyone who values the sanctity of human life should stand with me. I hope I may count on you, Lady Harriet, to use your influence with the members of Parliament now that you have resumed your salons."

As Caroline placed her hand on Lord Westwood's sleeve, Harriet forced herself to look at Mr. Wilberforce. "You have always had my support," she assured him. "Indeed, sir, I have repeatedly offered you the opportunity to address our little gatherings, but you have always declined."

"I know." He sighed wearily. "Most of my evenings are

spent in writing and, I confess, resting from the demands of my days. All this traveling is a bit fatiguing at my age. Sometimes I despair of living to see slavery abolished, but just as I reach my lowest point, I realize there is more I can do." He hesitated. "I understand that Lord Castlereagh has consented to attend your salon on Thursday next." To her amazement, Mr. Wilberforce blushed.

Harriet smiled. "Dear Mr. Wilberforce, if you are trying to wangle an invitation, say no more. I will send one around in the morning. It would be my great honor."

"You are too kind, Lady Harriet, though I have handled this awkwardly." He gave her an apologetic smile, then bowed. I fear I am not at my best at society balls. If you will excuse me—"

"Even your worst is a delight, sir," Harriet replied gallantly. "I look forward to seeing you next week." She smiled fondly at Mr. Wilberforce as he took his leave. Her next salon was shaping up to be a lively and important event. It was what she enjoyed most—bringing together men and women of disparate views in the hope that exchanging those views would result in a positive change. Many in power thought that their way was best, that change was unnecessary. But a leader who remained locked in the past was incapable of crafting a vision for the future. Her salons were designed to foster open-mindedness and tolerance of conduct that others might be quick to condemn.

Such as the sudden disappearance from the party of her betrothed and Freddy's former mistress.

Harriet frowned. If Lord Westwood wished to take the air with Caroline, it should not disturb her in the least. Nevertheless, as she stared at the spot where they had stood in such a friendly fashion not moments ago, it disturbed her a great deal.

And before she could truly examine the reason, Harriet found herself crossing the ballroom, ignoring the greetings that came her way as her gaze fixed on the large double doors that led out onto Lady Symington's secluded terrace.

Her pulse pounded in her ears, blocking out everything but those beckoning doors and the black swath of night that lay beyond.

Elias was lazily contemplating the front of Lady Forth's gown. She had a way of toying with the bodice that made the neckline gape provocatively, drawing attention to her extraordinary breasts. All the while, she regarded him with wide-eyed innocence, as if she thought he would find the combination of innocence and seductive allure irresistible.

He would, perhaps—in a woman whose innocence was genuine, not a carefully staged act. Lady Forth had obviously marked him as her next conquest. Normally, Elias did not mind that sort of game. He wondered why this one irritated him.

"I find the night air most stimulating," Lady Forth said in a husky tone as she studied a potted rubber tree at the edge of the terrace. Her fingers played with the pearls that disappeared into the shadowy area between her breasts.

"Do you?" Elias gave her a coolly assessing gaze.

As Lady Forth turned to him, she straightened her bodice, which afforded him an even closer view of her charms. "I am a notoriously poor sleeper, my lord. I am at my best long after others have retired."

The woman might as well wear a sign advertising her services. "And is Lord Forth a night owl as well?" Elias asked blandly.

Lady Forth sighed. "My husband prefers to keep to the country, where he rises with the chickens and goes to bed at an obscenely early hour. The country does not suit me. We have therefore come to an accommodation. I keep my own hours in town, while he remains in the country. It is an equitable arrangement, do you not think?"

"Certainly a convenient one."

Smiling, she nodded. "One does grow lonely. As a man who travels, you must find that to be true."

"One compensates with various amusements."

"Yes."

She moved closer. The front of her gown brushed his sleeve. She did not try to make the contact appear accidental. Instead, she inclined her face upward, a clear invitation in her eyes. Her lashes fluttered shut as she waited for his kiss.

Dispassionately, Elias studied her. Lady Forth was a beautiful woman. Her plump lips were ready for the taking. Doubtless, she indeed offered a cornucopia of sensual delights during those illicit, late-night hours. And though she did not make the blood rush to his head in a dizzying wave of wonder, it was certainly flowing to another, more responsive part of his anatomy.

He bent his face to hers. Her lips parted eagerly.

And in that moment, lush with sultry promise, something heavy and unpleasant struck Elias's arm with the force of a dead weight. With a little shriek, Lady Forth jumped back—just as a large, shiny object thrust itself into the rapidly enlarging space between them.

It was a rubber leaf, heralding the fall of the tree itself. The enormous potted plant toppled to the ground, landing at Elias's feet with a resounding crash. His gaze shot to the edge of the terrace, where it had stood. To his amazement, Lady Harriet now occupied the spot.

"Oh, dear! I am so sorry!" His fiancée looked stricken. "I did not see that little shrub. I'm afraid that I tripped and knocked it over."

Elias eyed the unwieldy tree at his feet. "An unobtrusive little bush, to be sure," he observed dryly.

Lady Forth, to her credit, looked only a bit rattled. "Harriet, dear," she managed. "How good it is to see you again. My felicitations on your betrothal."

"Thank you, Caroline." Lady Harriet's gaze moved from Elias to Lady Forth and back to him.

An awkward silence descended. Elias cleared his throat, but did not speak. Lady Forth peered at them over the tips of the rubber tree leaves. "Well," she said at last, "you will excuse me for not staying to chat, Harriet. Lord Westwood was kind enough to escort me out here to take the air, but I believe the night has taken a chilly turn."

With a perfunctory smile, Lady Forth walked inside the house, apparently not the least disconcerted at being caught in a provocative position with another woman's fiancé. Clearly, it would take more than a rubber tree to faze Lady Forth.

Standing in the shadows, Lady Harriet wore an unreadable expression. Elias thought her lips trembled a bit, but it was impossible to tell. Again he cleared his throat. "I expect I should apologize," he began.

Immediately, she bent over the tree, busying herself with the task of trying to set the pot upright. "There is no need," she assured him.

"I was on the point of kissing another woman," he pointed out.

"That is your own business, my lord." She pulled hard on the plant, but its weight was more than she could manage easily. She bit her lip.

With one hand, Elias reached down and set the tree aright. "Many women would object to finding their betrothed kissing another woman."

"Yes, I suppose so. But ours is not a real betrothal. You owe me no special loyalty."

That was exactly the thought that had run through Elias's head when he had strolled outside with Lady Forth—and what he would have told Lady Harriet if she had dared to challenge him. The fact that she did not was vaguely disturbing.

"You did not mind that Lady Forth and I conducted ourselves in a manner that could have made you the object of public ridicule?" He eyed her incredulously. Their betrothal might be a sham, but all of London thought it real. Had the scandalous tete-à-tete been discovered, Lady Harriet would have been humiliated. He wished he had thought of that before escorting Lady Forth outside.

She studied her slippers. "I do not set myself up as judge of other people's behavior."

"You merely throw trees at them."

Looking up, she flushed. "That was an accident. I would never do such a thing on purpose!"

"No. You are never upset. I had almost forgotten. Was Lady Forth Freddy's mistress?"

Shock registered on her face. "Y-y-yes, she was," she stammered.

"You knew all along."

"What does that matter? Many men had other interests outside of marriage." Her chin set defiantly. "I see no point in discussing it."

"And you bear the lady no ill will," he probed ruthlessly, his voice dripping with sarcasm.

"That is not quite true." Her candor surprised him. "I was glad she made him happy, but I do wish she had not been quite so . . . diligent in her efforts to please him. Freddy was not well. He would have done better to come home that night, instead of going to her. She should have seen that."

"That night?" Elias stared at her. "Do you mean that Lady Forth was—"

"The last person to see Freddy alive," she confirmed. "He died in her arms. I suppose he died pleasurably, but I have never been able to look at Caroline in quite the same way since then."

"I see." It was a miracle that Lady Harriet had not thrown ten rubber trees at them. "I am sorry," he added lamely.

Her too-bright smile almost made him cringe. "Thank you, my lord. And now, perhaps you would care to return to the party. I believe Caroline was right. The night has grown chilly."

"I will take you home."

"Oh, no." She eyed him in surprise. "We have not had supper yet. And I do not want her to think—" She broke off, embarrassed.

"You do not want to give Lady Forth the satisfaction of knowing that she has caused you distress. That is understandable. But she did cause you pain, and I see no need for you to remain and continue to endure it."

Elias put an arm around her waist and steered her toward the house. "I will make our excuses."

"I am not the sort of woman to leave a party early claiming a headache," she insisted. "I do not give in to weakness."

"Perhaps it is time you did."

"I did not give you leave to order me about, Lord Westwood," she protested as he pulled her through the ballroom in search of their hostess.

Elias did not respond. Lady Harriet had some devilish queer ideas, but he was not about to stand here all night and watch her suffer. For her own good, someone needed to take the woman in hand. It would have to be him.

As it turned out, she made very little protest in the end. By the time the carriage rolled away from Lady Symington's, she had lapsed into silence. But the stubborn set of her chin and the tightness of her features told him that while he may have won this little skirmish, he had by no means won the battle.

Had she really shoved that rubber tree at them? It was quite possible that she had tripped and sent it sprawling, but the pot and tree together must have weighed nearly four stone. It would have taken a determined push to move it.

Elias wondered why Lady Harriet was so insistent on disavowing her passions. To be sure, he often struggled to master his own very volatile temper. But he had never denied its existence.

Had her marriage proved so very disappointing that she must hide her rage beneath platitudes about not judging others? Elias could well imagine that Freddy had been a trial. He had met Freddy at school years ago. Then, as later, Freddy had been a scamp—albeit a harmless one—and a hapless gambler. When Freddy had come into a large sum of money six years ago, he had happily invested in Elias's business, which quickly showed a good return. Since Freddy was content to let Elias make the business decisions, the partnership had worked perfectly—until Freddy had had the stupidity to die in Lady Forth's arms.

Elias did not understand why Freddy had felt the urge to stray. Lady Harriet was infinitely more interesting than the manipulative Lady Forth. He wondered what had gone wrong between them. Had a lack of children been a factor? After all, they had been married for five years.

Something niggled at him. Six years ago, at the time of Freddy's wedding, Elias had been in the West Indies, purchasing plantations with what was left of his own funds. He had never met Freddy's bride, nor questioned his assumption that Freddy's sudden infusion of funds derived from gambling successes.

But Freddy never had any gambling successes. He was as inept at the cards as any man Elias had known.

Now he understood what bothered him. The money that rescued his business had come from Lady Harriet's dowry.

Lady Harriet, not Freddy, had made Westwood Imports possible, however unwittingly. And while Elias had reaped handsome profits, the return on her investment had been a faithless husband.

"I will take some brandy, thank you."

Harriet did not recall offering Lord Westwood brandy. Indeed, all she wanted was to retire to her room in peace and try to recover from the hellish evening.

He eyed her expectantly. The man was probably famished. Thanks to her, they had missed Lady Symington's late supper. But Harriet could offer him little in the way of a meal. Celestial had the night off, and Heavenly had gone to Kensington to visit a friend. Horace was probably around somewhere, but he was of no use in the kitchen.

"I regret depriving you of your dinner, my lord. Let me go into the kitchen and find us some food." Harriet put her reticule down on the hall table. Her thoughts were a jumble, for the image of Lady Forth's lovely face turned up to Lord Westwood's, awaiting his kiss, lingered vividly in her mind. Fortunately, she did not have to think in order to produce a meal. She poured him some brandy and made for the kitchen. To her surprise, he followed her.

"Your kitchen is my favorite room," he explained.

It was hers, too. Harriet had never held with the fashionable practice of relegating the kitchen to the basement. The food from such a kitchen never arrived hot. A damp, airless basement was a place for laundry, not culinary inspiration. Remodeling Freddy's town house so that the kitchen and dining room were just a corridor away had been one of her first acts as his wife. Perhaps that fact spoke volumes about their marriage, Harriet thought ruefully.

Tonight she was grateful for her airy, cheerful kitchen, for it somehow felt like the perfect place to entertain a man with Lord Westwood's appreciation of food. The stove had long since grown cold, but wine-roasted gammon, fruit, and baguettes left over from last night's meal would make a perfect cold buffet. Lord Westwood perched on a stool as she set the ham on a platter and prepared to carve the joint.

"Let me." He took the knife from her hand and performed a masterful job of carving.

They ate companionably at the table where the servants usually took their meals. Lord Westwood did not look a bit out of place, even in his elegant double-breasted corbeau coat and cream breeches, but Harriet felt awkward in her taffeta gown, which rustled audibly whenever she moved.

"Wine-roasted," he observed, savoring the gammon like a connoisseur. "Madeira, perhaps?"

In spite of her mood, Harriet smiled. "Yes. You have quite a talent, my lord."

"I have a talent for committing faux pas." He leveled a gaze at her. "I am sorry about what happened tonight."

Harriet paled. She did not want to talk about *that.* "Your apology is unnecessary, my lord."

"Because you are an excessively tolerant woman?"

"You imply that tolerance is a character flaw," Harriet retorted. "The truth is, there is far too much intolerance these days."

Lord Westwood speared another piece of ham. "Handing over your husband, and now your betrothed, to another woman is tolerance in the extreme, madam."

Harriet's gown rustled as she drew herself up. "I have never handed any man to Lady Forth," she corrected indignantly. "It pleases her to take them."

"Oh, I daresay that after tonight she might think twice," he drawled. "Tell me—did you ever toss a rubber tree at her and Freddy?"

"That was an accident!" Harriet threw her hands out in frustration. "Why do you not believe me?"

"What I believe," he said quietly, "is that you are a woman of many parts—most of which do not know what the other parts are about."

Harriet stared at him.

"You profess tolerance," he continued, "yet in your jealousy, you fling potted plants—"

"*Jealousy!* How dare you, sir! Such . . . such hubris!"

He gave her a long look. "You deny your own passions,

and yet you seem possessed of so many that you lose all control."

Harriet jumped to her feet. "I have never in my life lost control," she said fiercely.

"I imagine that is what makes it so difficult."

His gaze held a glimmer of sympathy. Harriet turned away so that she would not see it. After a moment, he continued. "For many years, my temper got the better of me. I was forever smashing things, injuring myself and others as I gave vent to my rage. But in the military I learned that to give in to rage, to lose control, is to risk death. Only cool heads prevail in war. And so I taught myself to control my temper." He paused. "But I have paid a price."

Curiosity banished her own anger. Harriet waited for him to explain.

"In the world of business it is likewise necessary to maintain one's composure and ability to reason. Lady Harriet, you are looking at a man who has successfully subjugated emotion to pragmatism." He cocked his head consideringly. "And who has been royally bored."

And then he grinned, a slow curve of his lips that took her breath away. She had been right—there *was* a dimple, there in his left cheek. Feeling inexplicably weak, Harriet sank into her seat, mesmerized by that sensual smile and the dark, swirling currents in his eyes.

"That is the price I have paid for control," he said in a matter-of-fact tone. "The problem you face is somewhat different."

"It . . . it is?"

"Yes. I have given the matter some thought. I recognize my anger, but refuse to give into it. You deny its existence—indeed, the existence of all passion. That is why you open your house to such blathering creatures—"

"I beg your pardon!"

"—Why you smile brightly as another woman tries to

seduce your betrothed; why you busy yourself with such ridiculously inappropriate activities as that bakery—"

"*Ridiculous!* How dare you!"

"—Why you ceded your husband to another woman without so much as a struggle. You wish to avoid facing the truth: that you are a woman of unbridled, tempestuous emotion."

Harriet struggled to maintain her poise. There was an odd ringing in her ears, and she suspected it stemmed from something akin to raw fury. "I must ask you to leave," she said in a constricted voice.

He seemed unperturbed. "I will help you. As it happens, I am obliged to you, for your dowry provided Freddy's investment in Westwood Imports. I will therefore show you how to rid your life of its trying distractions."

"The only trying distraction I face at the moment is you, my lord." Harriet removed Lord Westwood's plate, though it still held a quantity of food. "Your hat is in the hall," she said pointedly.

Nimbly, he snatched one last piece of ham from the plate. "Your life is in shambles, Lady Harriet. I will help you set things aright. We will start with the salons—unnecessarily agitating. You cannot manage such stress. Henceforth, I will review the guest list before the invitations are sent."

"Lord Westwood." Harriet put one hand on his sleeve and the other on her suddenly pounding head.

"Yes?" He eyed her tolerantly.

"Get out of my house."

The kitchen stood empty. A pregnant silence filled the darkness, followed by two long sighs of relief.

Celestial emerged from behind the pantry door, where she had slipped when the voices of Lady Harriet and Lord Westwood had drifted toward the kitchen. Then Horace stepped out, rubbing his arms stiffly. He pulled a deck of cards from his pocket.

"I had a good hand," he groused, staring at the cards. "I don't know why we had to hide like common criminals. For damned near three quarters of an hour, too. I'm so stiff I can hardly move."

"We were in the way. They needed to be alone."

"Hmmph! As if that's going to accomplish anything. They were at each other's throats."

"Not the whole time," Celestial put in.

"Time enough. If you think those two have a prayer of staying together, you are daft, woman. I give that betrothal three weeks."

Celestial regarded him thoughtfully. "I think he is attracted to her."

"Of course he's attracted to her," Horace replied impatiently. "Lady Harriet is a damned lovely woman. A man would be dicked in the nob not to want a woman like that. But it don't mean he has to marry her."

"I think Lady Harriet is drawn to him, too." Celestial giggled. "Just imagine! She threw a tree at him and Lady Forth."

"That means nothing. Women want only what they can't have."

Celestial's smile faded. "Whatever makes you think that?"

"A lifetime of learning, that's what. Women can't be trusted. They lead you a merry dance that ends soon enough when the band stops playing."

"Do you think all women are like that?"

Horace shot her a wary gaze. "Not all, I suppose. You're a right enough one. But we've known each other for years. And there isn't anything between us."

"No," Celestial quickly agreed. She hesitated. "It was rather stuffy behind the door all that time, wasn't it?"

Horace ran his finger around the inside of his collar. "I'll say. Wasn't hardly enough room to breathe."

Celestial lowered her lashes. "Yes, it was very close. I am sorry you were so uncomfortable."

Horace did not speak. Nervously, he began to shuffle the cards in one hand. The silence between them grew.

"I did not mind it as much as you," she said at last.

He stared at her.

Celestial took a deep breath and met his gaze. "I find your presence very comforting, Horace. And . . . stimulating."

"Stimulating?" A card fluttered to the floor. Quickly, Horace bent down to retrieve it. But as he rose, Celestial plucked the card from his hand. Calmly, she took the rest of the deck from his other hand. As their fingers touched, Horace froze.

Celestial set the cards on the table beyond his immediate reach, but Horace had no thought of recovering them. His feet were rooted to the spot.

"Do you think you could bring yourself to kiss me, Horace?" Celestial asked softly.

Horace blinked. "Oh, I don't know, Celestial. We have never—"

"No, we haven't," she agreed. "But could you, do you think?"

"Could I what?"

"Kiss me." She turned her face up to his.

Horace swallowed hard. "I . . . maybe."

Celestial's lips parted slightly, encouragingly, as she moved closer. "This isn't proper," Horace protested. "After all these years, I don't think—"

"That is right, Horace," she said, gently pulling his face down to hers. "Don't think."

Chapter Nine

"Beggin' your pardon, my lord, but you never did learn to tie a cravat properly." Henry eyed the pile of rumpled muslin at Elias's feet.

With a sound of disgust, Elias threw his latest effort on the floor. "Spare me the lecture, Henry. I grew tired of waiting for you to return."

"I was only gone for a moment," Henry protested.

"A moment to press the jacket, half an hour to gossip with the footmen. I ought to hire a housekeeper. She would get far more work out of those two. And you, for that matter."

Henry drew himself up. "The day a female has free rein in this household is the day—"

"Enough." Elias waved a dismissive hand. Despite the difficulties with his cravat, he was in too good a mood to listen to one of Henry's tirades. "See if you can discipline this into something presentable." He handed Henry another length of muslin and absently began to hum.

Casting Elias a speaking look, Henry proceeded to fashion the fabric into an intricate emblem of his rank. Henry had been with him for so long that Elias did not know what he would do without the man—even though he occasionally put his nose where it did not belong.

Last night, for example, Henry had been very curious as to why Elias had returned early from Lady Symington's ball, especially since the countess was known to set a very fine dinner table. Being Henry, he had not hesitated to remark upon the subject.

" 'Tis not like you to turn down a chance at lobster patties," Henry had pointed out. "No doubt she had Gunther's prepare a special dessert—"

"I had a perfectly adequate meal." Elias was not about to confess that he had taken cold gammon and fruit in Lady Harriet's kitchen and considered it a meal beyond price.

Nor could he say why he felt like humming this morning, especially since she had virtually thrown him out of her house last night. He ought to be wallowing in the doldrums, for none of his plans had borne fruit: He had not charmed her, or seduced her, or made her his mistress. But he had made progress. He was very close to understanding what made Lady Harriet tick.

Her life held too much agitation. She needed to simplify—to reorder her existence so that it was not so frantic, so that she could understand and conquer her fear.

How had it taken him so long to recognize the truth, that Lady Harriet was deathly afraid of being hurt? She had deliberately kept herself busy during her marriage so as to block out the fact of Freddy's faithlessness. Now she was determined not to get close to any man lest her armor slip and leave her open to a mortal wound. She had learned that caring could be deadly.

She had forced him into this betrothal in order to master her own desires, to arm herself against passion so that she would never be weak and vulnerable again.

Elias knew the pain of rejection himself, for he had cared for Zephyr. But he had acknowledged his pain—if not to the world, at least to himself—whereas Lady Harriet preferred to bury hers. He hoped Freddy was being charred to a crisp in some eternal fire for causing her such misery. Freddy had been a poor example of the male species. And from what Elias had heard, that father of hers was no beacon of warmth either.

A two-pronged attack would work best, he decided, for a target forced to defend itself on two fronts almost never managed to do so successfully. Elias would remove the causes of her distraction and make her confront him as a man. Perhaps she had already begun to do so; despite her denials, nothing less than jealousy could have prompted her to toss a rubber tree at him and Lady Forth.

He would not let Lady Harriet deny her desire. No one should be ruled by fear, least of all a woman made for passion. He would get her life on the right track. He owed her that, because of her dowry, the dowry that had helped start his business.

Oh, yes—his business, and the shares. He would get the shares. He was not worried about that.

With a final check of his cravat, Elias nodded at Henry and left his chamber to start his day.

Frowning, Henry stared after him. His lordship had been humming. That was a bad sign. Lord Westwood never hummed—except when there was a woman. Not just any woman, either. An image of Miss Zephyr Payne sprang unbidden to Henry's mind. Miss Payne had made Lord Westwood hum.

He ought to have taken his lordship's betrothal to Lady Harriet more seriously. Henry had assumed it was part of his employer's scheme to regain control of his business, for the earl was a practical man and would do what was necessary to achieve his goal. A temporary betrothal in the name of restoring his business was entirely acceptable.

But humming was not good. Humming meant that Henry's life might very well change, and not for the better.

He was not about to take the chance that this betrothal

might turn into a wedding or that he, Henry Milton, would end up in a house with women.

Drastic action was called for. The sort of action that he had resorted to once before, with stunning success. First, he would have to find out more about Lady Harriet Worthington and her friends.

"I have had a letter from Squire Gibbs," Monica told her. "Oh, Harriet, I wish I were back in Sussex. London is too busy. Eustace has not been home three nights in a row. What does he do with himself, I wonder?"

"What all young men his age do," Harriet replied. "Do not worry. Eustace has more than his share of common sense. He has grown into a man, you know."

Monica sighed. "I shall have to accept that fact, I suppose, but it is hard. For years I have done nothing but fuss over Eustace. I do not know what I shall do now."

Harriet eyed the missive lying in her friend's lap. "What does Cedric have to say?"

"He implores me to try to persuade you to sell the mill." She paused. "And he allows that the country is very thin of company. I think he misses you."

"Me?" Harriet laughed. "Not a chance."

"He wanted to marry you, Harriet."

"He wanted to possess my mill," Harriet corrected. "In Cedric's universe, marriage is the only way to bend a recalcitrant female to his will. It is a very masculine way of looking at things."

"Obviously, he has had to abandon that strategy, since he thinks you betrothed to Lord Westwood. But he still needs a mother for all those children." Monica shook her head. "Poor things."

Harriet slanted an assessing gaze at her friend. "I have thought about employing Cedric to oversee the mill and the crops, perhaps even the bakery. It is all a bit much for me. He knows that business better than anyone in Sussex, but I do not know whether his pride would let him accept the job, and on my terms."

"He is a proud man," Monica conceded. "The children are driving him to distraction, and he sometimes drowns his troubles in drink. But beneath it all, Mr. Gibbs is a worthy man."

"If only I could be certain that he would abide by my wishes. I will not have him forcing prices up again. The mill is for everyone, regardless of their ability to pay."

"His family has run the mill for generations," Monica pointed out. "Perhaps he is not to be blamed for expecting things to continue in the same fashion."

Harriet regarded her friend closely. Monica's life had been lonely after her husband's abandonment, and she had filled it with devotion to Eustace. Harriet had the distinct impression that her friend wished only to be back in the country, nurturing someone who needed her. But although Harriet wanted Monica to be happy, she did not want loneliness to propel her into a desperate decision she would later regret.

"Do I gather that you have been corresponding frequently with Cedric?"

Monica flushed. "I do not think he writes me for any reason other than he knows I have your ear."

"There is one way to find out." Abruptly, Harriet sat down at her writing table and began to compose a letter.

"What are you doing?"

"I am writing to offer Cedric the position we discussed. I will invite him to visit me in London to discuss my proposal. I shall ask him to stay here. Should you mind?"

Monica looked startled. "Why should I mind?"

"No reason." Harriet smiled. "I merely thought it prudent to ask."

"Eustace will be thrilled," Monica quickly added. "He enjoys Mr. Gibbs's company."

Harriet tactfully refrained from pointing out Eustace and Cedric had never had two words to say to each other.

"This is nothing but a bunch of rabble-rousers and ne'er-do-wells." Clearly appalled, Lord Westwood regarded the guest list scornfully.

"Mr. Wilberforce is not a ne'er-do-well," Harriet retorted. "Or do you hold with slavery, my lord? I imagine those plantations of yours are worked—"

"By paid laborers," he snapped. "I abolished slavery on my property long ago."

Harriet ignored him, as it did not suit her to make peace with this maddeningly interfering man. "And pray, into which category does Lord Castlereagh fall, rabble-rouser or ne'er-do-well?"

He shrugged. "A statesman or two does not mask the fact that they will sit cheek and jowl with radicals and bedlamites."

"Mr. Hazlitt is a very respected critic," Harriet said. "and Mr. Shelley has done nothing more shocking than to elope—"

"With that very strange young woman," Lord Westwood finished. "But more to the point: How can you think of having Hunt back after his rudeness on the last occasion?"

"I see. Mr. Hunt is the root of your difficulty. You did not like the way he challenged you, and so your solution is never to go anywhere he is expected to be."

"Nonsense. I simply dislike how you turn your house over to the likes of—"

"And here I thought you held your own with him so admirably," Harriet put in sweetly. "Little did I suspect that you were a coward at heart."

Lord Westwood's scowl would have terrified a timid woman, but Harriet merely ignored his darkening features. "I am not afraid of you, my lord. Nor shall I rescind any of my invitations simply because you do not wish to submit yourself to an evening of lively discourse."

"Lively discourse?" He scoffed. "More like the rantings of lunatics."

Harriet glared at him. Lord Westwood had ruined her afternoon. He had sent a curt note around this morning announcing that he would present himself at three o'clock to review the list for tomorrow night's salon. He had appeared right on time, and they had spent the better part of an hour quarreling. The man was arrogant in the extreme. How dare he try to change her guest list?

"These are my friends," she insisted with a defiant toss of her head. But an errant tendril of hair slipped its pins and floated into her face, quite spoiling the effect of her firm declaration. Harriet tucked the stray tendril behind her ear. "You are free to go elsewhere tomorrow night—although in that event I will assume you do not want your precious shares badly enough to continue the masquerade."

His features grew rigid. "I find you impossible, madam."

"Likewise, my lord."

Dark kernels of midnight glinted in the dangerous gaze that locked with hers. The atmosphere in the parlor thickened ominously. A shiver rippled Harriet's spine as she studied Lord Westwood's brooding countenance. She had the distinct impression that she had pushed him too hard. Harriet tried to suppress the frisson of fear that shot through her. He had a temper, but he could control it. Had he not said so? *Lady Harriet, you are looking at a man who has successfully subjugated emotion to pragmatism.*

Emotion ran rampant over his features now, however. His eyes held shards of hot fury. His jaw clenched into a rigid length of granite. His lips curled dangerously. If Lord Westwood was waging a battle for self-control, he was losing it.

Abruptly, he ripped the guest list in half, and threw it onto the writing table.

"My lord!" Harriet protested. But she spoke to his back, for he was already halfway to the parlor door.

"Come," he barked over his shoulder.

Such nerve! With all the disdain she could muster, Harriet managed a scornful laugh. "I am not going anywhere with you," she declared. That would put him in his place.

Then he turned, and she knew she had deluded herself. His expression was thunderous. Before she could fathom his intentions, he strode to her side, lifted her into his arms, and carried her out into the hall. Harriet tried to struggle, but he gripped her like an iron vise.

Heavenly descended the stairs in time to see Lord Westwood carry a wriggling, protesting Harriet out the front door. "Stop!" Heavenly cried, horrified.

Ignoring her, Lord Westwood tossed Harriet into his waiting curricle and jumped up beside her. With a crack of the whip, the carriage shot out of the drive. Heavenly turned to Horace, who was watching the little drama from his position at the doorway. "Fetch Bow Street—fetch someone!"

Calmly, Horace closed the door. "He'll bring her back when he's ready."

"When he's ready!" Heavenly stared at him in disbelief. "Are you daft? The man is abducting her!"

"He's just showing her what's what," Horace replied. "Celestial and I think Lord Westwood has the right of it. He's going to help her."

Heavenly sank onto the bottommost step of the staircase, her jaw agape.

What sort of persuasion worked with a woman as stubborn as Lady Harriet? Perhaps he should have asked himself that question before he made off with her, but Elias had run out of patience in the exact moment she had toyed with that errant lock of hair in a way that made his blood boil with anger or passion or something in between. Whatever it was, it had overtaken him. Sometimes a man had to act, and persuasion be damned.

The clip-clop of the horses' hooves droned on, their steady beat accentuating the thundering of his own pulse. Elias had no idea where they were. He had lost his sense of time and place. Only his nose seemed to function as it picked up the heady scent of wildflowers.

With every ounce of his will, Elias tried to clear the fog from his brain. He ventured a glance at Lady Harriet, who grimly clutched the seat, not bothering to shield her hair from the wind that swept it into a swirl of auburn tangles. Their swift departure had not permitted her the luxury of fetching a hat, and now her hair was a mess. Once he would have found such unkemptness off-putting. Now he could only stare at that auburn mass and imagine that it would look just like this when they made love. He would run his hands through it as he—

No, he must not allow such thoughts.

With iron discipline, Elias willed the image away. Slowly, the fog in his mind began to clear; the pounding in his veins subsided. At last he focused on the scenery that rushed past them. London's brick and stone had given way to oak and heather. Good God. They must be halfway to Uxbridge by now.

Damnation. He had sent them barreling down the Oxford Road with no particular destination in mind merely because once more she had gotten the best of him.

What in God's name was he doing?

Pulling back on the reins, Elias directed the horses into a clearing at the side of the road. When the curricle rolled to a stop under the shade of a tall oak tree, Elias took a deep, calming breath. His world had turned upside down. He had lost control, all because of the woman beside him who did not realize her own sensual power, who bristled like a porcupine when he tried to make her face her fears.

He had not lost his temper in a very long time. No woman had ever pushed him beyond the limits of his control. Shaken, Elias got out of the curricle and looped the reins around a branch. He glanced at Lady Harriet. She was still clutching the seat. She looked stiff, uncompromising, and angry as a wet hen.

Elias did not try to cajole her out of the curricle. Instead, he placed his hands around her waist, which drew from her a startled little shriek, and lifted her down. As he set her on the ground, he saw fury in her eyes.

"Lady Harriet," he began wearily, "I wish to apologize for—"

Her palm connected with the side of his face. The sound of the blow reverberated in the otherwise silent clearing. Elias stared at her. To his amazement, her blue eyes filled with fear and regret. She cringed, almost as if she expected him to hit her back.

With a helpless shake of his head, Elias pulled her into his arms.

She flailed at him for all of three seconds, then went limp with defeat as the fury went out of her. She looked scared, helpless. Elias felt her trembling as he brought his lips to hers in a gentle, restrained kiss. He had no right even to such a sedate kiss, not after he had ripped her from the safety of her home because he had not been man enough to control his temper.

But he had to taste that sweet mouth. His nerves felt raw and ragged, and he could not deny himself. He tilted her head up and kissed her again. And again.

It was not enough.

Soft and gentle kisses inflicted excruciating torment on him that did not begin to fill the need within. Rage had drained everything from him, leaving only a bottomless chasm that could not be satiated by anything less than raw, bone-rattling passion. Elias tried to restrain himself, but for the first time he understood the limits of his control. Empty of all save wanting her, he had to brand her with the wild passion that rose in him like fear. His tongue forced itself between her lips, and his hands buried themselves in that delightful mass of auburn hair.

Even as he gained the warmth of her mouth, regret pierced his soul. He had to stop, to salvage his honor and hers. He was not a barbarian, though he felt like one. With every fiber of his being shrieking in rebellion, Elias forced himself to release her. His hands dropped uselessly to his sides.

Her limpid blue eyes opened wide. For a long, breathtaking moment their gazes held. And then, to his amazement, she stood up on her toes and kissed him full on the lips.

Something in him soared to the heavens. Longing and lust surged anew. His mind filled with wonder at her unexpected responsiveness.

Wrapping her arms around his neck, she pressed against him as if her very life depended upon it. Her lips parted, inviting his invasion with a willingness that stunned him. And when his shameless hands began to roam over her, she answered with a moan of sheer pleasure.

Her knees buckled. Elias supported her weight for a moment and then laid her gently down in the soft clover. The curricle shielded them from the view of any passersby, but Elias could not have cared less. He wanted Lady Harriet Worthington, Freddy's maddeningly tolerant widow, more than he had ever wanted anything in his life.

And still she did not speak.

The delicate fragrance of primrose hit him as he nuzzled against her neck. It was hers, this flower. He would never smell it again without thinking of her. Primrose and clover, the sweet smells of desire.

Elias trailed kisses from her neck down to her shoulders. He pushed her bodice away so that he could kiss her there, too. He heard her gasp of surprise and delight as his tongue touched the tip of her breast.

She arched upward, teasing and pleading at the same time. He thought he would explode with wanting her. The knowledge that she wanted him too was the final spark to his need. With a groan, Elias covered her body with his. He kissed her lips, her chin, her cheeks. His hands went to either side of her head and tangled in the auburn curls.

This was how he had envisioned her from the first moment in the bakery, he realized. Lying with him in some perfumed meadow, her hair fanning out from her flushed face, her eyes reflecting the glory of her passion.

Then he saw the tears.

His heart slammed in his chest. Her eyes held desire, all right, but also shock. Her cheeks were flushed with passion—and mortification. Her lips trembled in longing—and dismay.

Tears splashed from her eyes like rain. She looked up at him with a mixture of fear and confusion and loathing, but she did not speak. She lay there, a silent portrait of wanton desire frozen by the heavy hand of regret.

Clover caught in her hair. Grass clung to her bare shoulders. Her breasts rose rapidly, and a sheen of perspiration clung to her skin. Her crumpled skirts were pushed halfway up to her waist. Her lips were swollen from his kisses.

Elias stared at all of this and knew, suddenly, that there were worse things than losing one's temper, than failing to win back his shares, than blundering in his scheme to reform Lady Harriet.

What was worse than all of that was the knowledge that he might, if he were not very careful, lose his heart to a woman as misguided as the ideological renegades who haunted her parlors. To a woman who loathed passion, and who even now—when she must have realized her own wanting—was looking at him with distaste.

She remained mute as he rearranged the fabric of her gown so that it covered her completely. He brushed away the grass and the clover and all signs of their lovemaking. Then he pulled her to her feet.

"Well, there you have it." His voice grated with the bitter tastes of unslaked passion and self-disgust. "A fine exhibition of desire. A perfect example of a man willing to make a fool of himself in the name of passion. Doubtless, you can use this lesson, madam, for your own edification."

As she regarded him in stunned silence, Elias handed her into the curricle and turned the vehicle around, toward London.

Chapter Ten

Such a thing had never happened to Harriet. Though she had known the intimacies of married life, her wildest dreams could not have imagined anything like yesterday afternoon in that meadow with Lord Westwood.

"Too much cream," Celestial announced.

"What?" Harriet stared at her blankly.

"You have too much cream in the filling. It won't hold together." Celestial's look said she knew exactly why Harriet's mind was wandering. Lord Westwood had created quite a stir in the household when he made off with her in such a commanding fashion.

His return had been much less conspicuous. In stony silence he had escorted her up the steps. When Horace opened the front door, Lord Westwood had turned and left without a word. Harriet had walked blindly to her room, not looking back, trying desperately not to cry. Sleep had not come for many hours.

"Now, Celestial," Harriet admonished wearily, "I know whether a filling will come together or no. It only wants beating. It is supposed to be rich, you know."

Celestial shrugged. "Rich is one thing. Killing a man with wretched excess is another."

Harriet stiffened. "Is there something you wish to say, Celestial?"

"Only that it's clear you and Lord Westwood had a

fight, and that you wish to make it up to him. I've never seen you concoct such a decadent thing." Celestial shot her a knowing gaze. "Funny how men will do that to you."

Harriet flushed. Celestial would not let the matter rest. None of them would. Horace—usually the soul of discretion—had eyed Harriet as if he could not believe his eyes. Heavenly had been badgering her all day for a full accounting of what had transpired yesterday afternoon.

"What goes on between me and Lord Westwood is no one's concern but mine," Harriet told Celestial firmly, determined not to be bullied by her own servants. "Now, let us get to work. We have dozens of these to make."

The inspiration for these little puff pastries had come to her overnight. Her restless sleep had brought dreams filled with a churning fire that licked at her insides and sparked wild fantasies. In one of them, she had been in the kitchen, creating decadent dishes for Lord Westwood's pleasure. As he watched her pile layer after layer of pastry and filling, his turbulent gaze hinted of savage appetites. Harriet had awakened trembling, thinking his hands were caressing her.

And though it had only been a dream, what he aroused within her was no dream. Harriet had spent most of her waking hours since yesterday trying to understand what about Lord Westwood rocked her to the core. She did not have an answer, but she did have her napoleons.

That is what she had decided to call them, for they had all the qualities of a coddled tyrant: rich and hard on the surface, pandering to greed and lust within. Her puff pastry promised the world—and delivered it in the lusty cream filling designed to make a man greedy for more.

Harriet desperately wanted Lord Westwood to like her napoleons, for she knew she had sorely disappointed him yesterday. She had let him make love to her, given rein to forces within her that wanted nothing more than to lie with him amid the clover. Then fear had swamped her.

The tears had come. His anger had been justified. He believed she was toying with him in the interest of mastering her own desire.

But she had not mastered it. Just the opposite, in fact. For though their betrothal was a sham, something between them was not a sham, something tantalizing and dangerous that drew her into a world of sensual delights. Harriet had stepped into the swirling waters of that world yesterday and frozen with fear. He had seen her longing and confusion and, like a fisherman measuring a catch that was not yet ready for the skillet, he had let her go.

But what about the next time? Would she have the strength to deny her desires?

Monica was right. She *was* ignorant of the world. She had been married, but she had never lost control in a man's arms nor driven a man to that state himself. Poor Freddy! She had given him so little. Every day she realized just how inferior had been her wifely skills.

Her party was tonight. Part of her could not wait until the moment Lord Westwood came through the door. The rest of her trembled in shame and wished him gone from her life forever.

Thank goodness she had signed that statement promising to end their betrothal.

"Sit still! I will never get these combs in." Heavenly stood over Harriet like a martinet. "I wish I knew what was going on around here."

"For the seventh time, Heavenly, there is nothing to tell. We drove out to the country, talked for a bit, and drove back."

"That accounted for all those grass stains on your gown, I suppose."

Harriet flushed. "I have done nothing that I am ashamed of." Which was not exactly the truth.

In response, Heavenly jerked the brush roughly

through her hair. Angrily, Harriet snatched it away. "You are too out of sorts to do this."

Heavenly gave a loud "hmmph" indicating her profound displeasure. "Things aren't right in this household," she grumbled. "With Celestial and Horace smelling of April and May and you making a fool of yourself over that lord—"

"Celestial and Horace?" Harriet was astonished. "Do you mean to say that they—"

"Yes." Heavenly crossed her hands over her chest and stared glumly at the floor.

"Celestial is entitled to her own life," Harriet said gently. "I know you must wish for her happiness."

"What about *my* happiness? If she leaves, I'm all alone."

"Why should she leave? If she and Horace marry, they can certainly remain in my employ."

Heavenly shook her head. "It won't be the same. Already, she hardly confides in me anymore. All she wants is to be with Horace." With a sigh, she regarded Harriet critically. "You look beautiful tonight. If that earl isn't nice to you, I'll come after him with my knitting needles. Oh, I almost forgot. This came."

The image of Lord Westwood dodging Heavenly's knitting needles almost made Harriet laugh—until she saw the note Heavenly thrust at her.

Dearest Lady Harriet,

You have been constantly in my thoughts. I know I ought not to speak of this, since you are betrothed to another, but I long to see you, to spend just one private moment in your luminous presence so that I can persuade you of my feelings. Please grant me that small request tonight. I remain truly yours, etc.

Oliver Hunt

Dear heavens. Mr. Hunt had never led her to believe he possessed such strong feelings. Perhaps she should not have taken that unsettling warmth in his eyes so lightly. But not tonight, dear lord, not tonight. With all the turmoil between her and Lord Westwood, Harriet did not think she could deal with Mr. Hunt or his feelings, whatever they might be.

Her long-planned salon suddenly appeared to be a disaster in the making.

Warily, Elias crossed the threshold of Lady Harriet's town house. As the butler took his hat, something flickered in the man's eyes. Elias caught another odd look from one of the other servants. Well, what did he expect? He had made a spectacle of himself yesterday.

Lady Harriet stood to the rear of the entrance, positioned to greet her guests. Seeing him, she flushed. Her obvious discomfiture gave Elias grim satisfaction. Let that be one more lesson she learned: Once two people behaved as they had done yesterday, there was hell to pay until they became lovers in earnest. The awkwardness, the longing, none of it would vanish until she walked willingly into his arms and submitted to him.

As he reached her side, a faint scent of wildflowers met his nostrils. It stirred his blood, fueling that spark of desire he had ruthlessly banked yesterday. He yearned to show her how they could enjoy each other once they got past the awkwardness. As usual, however, she was denying her passion. Despite the exotic capucine gown that brought out the fire in her hair, the smile pasted on her lips was as remote as an iceberg.

"Lady Harriet." The resonant baritone brought him up short. That fool Hunt was bowing over her hand as if it were the Holy Grail.

"M-M-Mr. Hunt," she stammered. Elias frowned.

What in Hunt's greeting had made her lose her composure?

"We have much to discuss," Hunt said in a low tone.

"Perhaps later." She reddened.

Had his ears been mistaken, or had Oliver Hunt just set the stage for an assignation with his fiancée? Such insolence was not to be tolerated. But before Elias could speak, Hunt moved away.

During the evening, Elias carefully watched the man and grew certain he was up to something. Hunt held forth in small groups with his usual arrogance, but his gaze often strayed to Lady Harriet.

Eustace was among those hanging onto Hunt's every word. Elias tried to recall whether he had gone through such a worshipful phase. At Eustace's age, he had already seen battle. There had been no time for idle pursuits—although he had followed one of his commanders around like a shadow, drinking in his every utterance on the strategies of war. So perhaps he had behaved a bit like Eustace.

Involved in his reverie, Elias only belatedly noticed that Mr. Hazlitt had taken offense at something Hunt said.

"I live to my own self, sir," Hazlitt growled. "I take a thoughtful interest in what is passing in the world, but I do not feel the slightest inclination to meddle in it."

"A man with your credentials would do better to turn your acclaim to good use," Hunt admonished. "How sad it is to see a man who wastes his celebrity in the cause of no one but himself when he could, if he wished, serve the public good. As I do."

"There is not a more mean, stupid, dastardly, pitiful, selfish, spiteful, envious, ungrateful animal than the public," Hazlitt retorted. "It is the greatest of cowards, for it is afraid of itself."

By now, the other conversations had stopped. Everyone gathered around the two men, one an acclaimed man of letters, the other noted for his revolutionary zeal. Wilberforce, the man Elias had seen conversing with Lady Harriet at Lady Symington's ball, spoke up.

"It is true that people are customarily afraid of change," Wilberforce said in a conciliatory tone. "And not all change is for the best, of course. But sometimes the public must be led to change because it will result in the greater happiness of others."

Hazlitt scoffed. "How little security we have when we trust our happiness to others!"

"My point exactly," Hunt snapped. "Many people have no security at all. Are you so blind, man, that you do not see?"

Studying Hunt's florid features, Elias found it hard to believe that this was the man who had so calmly skewered him the other night for his loyalty to the Crown. Tonight Hunt lacked the patience required for effective debate. He seemed agitated, almost preoccupied, and his attacks were more curt than considered.

"I see well enough that you, young man, have a love of power," Hazlitt replied disdainfully, "and therefore a love of yourself that will always take precedence over any charity you profess for that mewling public of yours."

Hunt rounded on Hazlitt, closing to within a whisker's breadth of the man. "You, sir, are an ass!"

"Better an ass than a fraud," Hazlitt spat out.

At Hunt's swift intake of breath, Elias heard fast bets being placed as to whether the two would come to fisticuffs. Ever the peacemaker, Wilberforce tried to intervene, but the two men simply ignored him. They glared at each other like two belligerent bulls.

"Do have a napoleon, gentlemen!" Lady Harriet darted between Hunt and Hazlitt with a platter. She thrust it upward, so that the confections entered their awareness precisely at the level of their mouths.

From his vantage point several feet away, Elias could

just make out the plump, enticing pastries. He had not seen their like before. He edged closer, but everyone else seemed to have the same idea. By the time he reached the platter, nary a one of the delicacies remained.

The argument was quickly forgotten. Everyone to a man was engaged in the act of polishing off the rich confections, which looked to have a brittle exterior interspersed with a cream filling.

Brittle on the outside, soft where it mattered. Like Lady Harriet.

Or perhaps not. Perhaps yesterday was an aberration never to be repeated. Perhaps she did not harbor any real desire for him, or any man. Perhaps she was cold and incapable of giving herself. Perhaps all that attention she lavished on every damned thing that came out of her kitchen was the only real passion that moved her.

Rejected for a cream puff. Was there anything more lowering?

"Mr. Hunt?" Harriet's uncertain gaze swept the shadows of the terrace. Instantly, a figure stepped out of the darkness.

"Harriet," he acknowledged in a velvet voice. "You do not mind that I call you Harriet, I hope?"

"I suppose not." Harriet looked around uneasily. It would not do for anyone to discover her engaged in a tete-à-tete with Oliver Hunt on the terrace. "What did you wish to see me about, sir?"

He moved closer. "I have thought of nothing else since yesterday, when I received your letter." He took her hand between his. "When you asked me for advice about your late husband's business concerns last fall, I had dared to hope you would eventually turn to me for something more intimate. I am not normally a patient man, but now I see that patience does indeed have its reward. I am touched and overwhelmed by your declaration."

"Letter?" Harriet wrinkled her brow in confusion. Last fall, when she had decided to sell Freddy's shares of Westwood Imports, her solicitor suggested that she mention the fact to her friends and acquaintances in order to stir up interest in the stock. Perhaps she had said something to Mr. Hunt, but such a conversation had held no special significance to her. She could not believe that he would have attached such weight to it.

"You write like an angel," Mr. Hunt said, pulling a piece of paper from his pocket, though in truth he had been rather surprised at her faulty grammar. "I shall treasure this missive until the day I die."

"Let me see that, sir." Harriet reached for the paper, but he jerked it away and caught her about the waist.

"So coy, so playful," he murmured, crushing her against his chest. "So delightful!"

Alarmed, Harriet tried to pull away. "You do not appear to be yourself tonight, Mr. Hunt. I daresay you have not been getting your rest, what with all your revolutionary activities." To her dismay, his arms locked more tightly around her.

"It is true that I have been engaged in important work." His sonorous voice deepened. "Revolutionary fervor can be unpredictable. Riots all over the country have demanded my attention."

"I can well imagine," Harriet replied politely, trying to pry his fingers from her waist. "It must be a great deal of work to channel the people's zeal to other areas."

"Oh, I am perfectly happy with their efforts. Rioting is the only way to get a recalcitrant government's attention. Only by creating mayhem can we accomplish anything. But it must be organized mayhem. It does no good to destroy something insignificant. Accordingly, I instruct my people in the importance of burning factories and storehouses, so as to gain the attention of the landed rich and putting even more pressure on the government."

Harriet eyed him in astonishment. "You condone such destruction?"

"I condone anything that leads to change. And I am delighted to have found a perfect helpmeet." He brought his lips to hers.

"Mr. Hunt, you have formed entirely the wrong impress—" Her words were cut off by his kiss.

"Lord Westwood."

Elias turned. He had been watching the door to the kitchen, wondering why Lady Harriet was taking so damned long to fetch more pastries. "Eustace," he acknowledged. "I trust you are well," he added politely.

"Well enough, my lord. Only—" Eustace halted, then stared down at his feet.

Elias almost felt sorry for the lad. He had not missed the troubled look in Eustace's eyes during Hunt's heated dispute with Hazlitt. Though a relentless iconoclast, Hazlitt had held his composure, whereas Hunt had revealed himself to be an intolerant, irrational bully.

Eustace looked downcast. Had the bloom faded from that particular rose? All to the good. Hunt was not worthy of Eustace's youthful adoration. "Do not take it so hard, Eustace. A true man does not need to belittle others to prove himself a man."

"Yes, sir. That is, I—" Eustace broke off in obvious frustration.

Elias eyed him in alarm. He fervently hoped that Eustace was not about to cry. "Why do we not go out on the terrace," he said quickly. Lady Harriet's pastries could wait a moment.

"Yes, the terrace." Eustace nodded vigorously. "That is just where we should go. I have been trying to tell you, but I think it is best if you see for yourself." To Elias's surprise, Eustace flushed a deep red.

"What the devil are you talking about?" Elias demanded, as Eustace pulled him through the parlor.

"Shhh!" Eustace admonished. "It would not do to attract attention. Come, my lord. Please hurry, or I fear it will be too late."

"Too late? For what?"

"Just hurry."

When they reached the terrace doors, Eustace fairly pushed him out into the night air.

At first, Elias thought they were alone. Then he picked out a muffled conversation in the vicinity of what he assumed was a normally silent bush.

"My dear, I will treasure this moment until I die," said an all-too-familiar baritone.

"And that moment, sirrah, is *now*!" Eustace shouted triumphantly in the direction of the shrubbery. He looked expectantly at Elias.

"What the—?" From behind the bush, a figure rose to his knees. Another figure sat up beside him.

"Eustace! Lord Westwood!" Lady Harriet's eyes were wide with wonder.

Elias registered her disheveled appearance and Hunt's proprietary air. Then he glanced at Eustace.

"This is what I was trying to tell you, Lord Westwood," Eustace replied, regarding Hunt with the look of a vengeful angel. "Do you wish to kill him now, or shall I have the honor of acting as your second?"

Elias's gaze returned to Hunt and Lady Harriet, who was hurriedly repairing the damage to her clothing. To his amazement, Hunt began to laugh.

"Go away, Eustace. You are bothering me. Rather like a pesky fly on the corn pudding. This is a matter between Lord Westwood and me—two *men,* not a mere pup."

Rage surged violently in Elias's breast. His fists clenched at his sides. His temple pounded. His muscles tensed. A throbbing fury threatened to blast from him like molten lava. He looked from Hunt to Lady Harriet, and all control slipped away.

"Yes, do leave us, Eustace." Her voice was trembling. "I do not think you a pup at all, but you must see that this is most embarrassing for me and I—oh, my!"

The sound of Elias's fist connecting with Hunt's jaw resounded through the night. In the next instant, Hunt lay prone at her feet.

Elias turned away. Strangely, he did not know why he had hit the man. Had it been on Eustace's behalf? Or hers?

It did not matter. He had to leave before he did something irrevocable, like wring her neck.

He had not gotten even one of those pastries.

Chapter Eleven

"You cannot go to his house!" Monica looked horrified.

"I must." Harriet picked up her reticule and walked past a gaping Horace, who had finally abandoned his effort to appear uninterested in matters involving his employer and Lord Westwood. "I cannot allow him to think I threw myself at Mr. Hunt."

"Mr. Hunt has apologized—quite prettily, I thought." Monica had rather enjoyed the spectacle of the proud Mr. Hunt groveling before them in the parlor this morning. "Perhaps he will even muster the courage to apologize to Lord Westwood, although I doubt it. The man seems to have little in the way of honor." Monica shook her head. "What does it matter, anyway? The betrothal is a sham. Why not let things be?"

"A *sham*?" Horace stared at them. "Did you say the betrothal is a sham?" No sooner were the words out than he clapped his hand over his mouth in mortification. "I beg your pardon, Lady Harriet," he said, reddening. "I should not have spoken. I do not know what has come over me lately."

"I suspect I do," Harriet said grimly. The normally reticent Horace had been turned inside out trying to satisfy Celestial's thirst for information. "Your concern—*everyone's* concern—is gratifying, but I must leave now."

Before Monica could protest further, Harriet swept out

the door. Determination gave her courage, but truth be told, she was as nervous as a cat. For the past two days, her efforts to reach Lord Westwood had met with stony silence. He had not responded to her note. He had not come around to escort her to the party they had been engaged to attend last night. Harriet could not abide his silence. His rage, perhaps, but not his silence.

She had never visited a gentleman at his house. It was not done, even by independent women, unless they wished to be taken for the gentleman's mistress. Harriet did not care about her reputation. She only knew she had to explain.

Eustace—who had apparently adopted Lord Westwood as his new hero—had said the earl was usually home in the afternoons. Eustace had been very helpful. Unlike Lord Westwood, he believed her protestations of innocence; he blamed Mr. Hunt for the incident on the terrace.

Harriet stood nervously on Lord Westwood's front steps. It occurred to her that for form's sake she should have asked Eustace to escort her here. But it was too late now. Besides, her errand was too personal, too private, too painful to be witnessed by a third party.

The manservant who answered Harriet's knock possessed all the warmth of an iceberg. He disappeared, and after what seemed like an eternity, returned with word that Lord Westwood would see her for five minutes. Harriet followed him through a musty corridor.

The house itself looked as if no one had lived in it for years. Harriet knew that Lord Westwood was often away, but she thought that someone should have set out a vase of flowers, at least, when he was in residence. Much of the furniture was draped in holland covers, adding to the air of disuse. Only the study into which Harriet was ushered lacked that stale, uninhabited atmosphere.

Lord Westwood presided at a massive desk, his hands resting lightly on a sheaf of papers. An open ledger book lay off to the side. His slightly distracted expression vanished the moment she crossed the threshold, to be replaced by a contemptuous glower. Harriet smiled brightly, but received no answering smile.

"I had to come, my lord." To her dismay, a quiver invaded her words.

"And so you are here. How may I help you?" His tone was cool, remote.

Since she had only five minutes, Harriet had no choice but to be direct. "Things were not at all what they appeared the other night. Mr. Hunt had sent me a note, or at least I thought he had. When he arranged that hasty rendezvous outside—"

"Hasty?" His gaze darkened. "Yes, that much was obvious. Though perhaps I would have said frantic. Or feverish. As if neither of you could wait."

Harriet flushed. "You mistook the situation."

"Oh? I suppose the two of you were not rolling around in the bushes like—"

"I tried to make him listen to reason, but he did not respond in the way I hoped," she interjected. "He pressed me into the bushes, and while I do not think he would have harmed me, I was very glad when you and Eustace arrived."

Those dark eyes were unreadable. Harriet was desperate to make him understand. "Mr. Hunt claimed that *I* had sent *him* a note, which I did not, my lord. This morning he denied sending me the note. So you see, someone tricked us both."

"Oh?" Now he looked bored. "Who might that be?"

Harriet shook her head. "I do not know. I only wish you did not think the worst of me."

"Does it matter what I think?"

"Yes."

"Why?"

Harriet could not think of an answer. Instead, she

reached into her reticule. "I made this for you. It is not as fresh as it was two days ago, but I hope you will accept it."

His gaze flicked over the napoleon.

"Orange blossoms."

"No, my lord," she corrected, surprised that his normally excellent sense of smell had failed him. "I used only cream and caster sugar, egg whites, and a few shavings from a vanilla bean."

"I was not referring to the pastry."

"Oh." Harriet thought hard, then blushed. "I . . I splashed on a bit of orange water this morning."

He arched a brow. "No primroses?"

You smell of flowers that grow by the side of the road, wild and free, daring anyone to pick them. Harriet had not forgotten his words. But she would have felt awkward wearing primrose today, as if she were trying to curry favor. "I . . . I thought the orange a nice change."

"I prefer primrose. You will wear that in the future."

Harriet stared at him.

Abruptly, Lord Westwood's forbidding expression vanished. He walked around the desk, took the napoleon from her hands, and set it aside. "I am glad you came."

"You are?" Harriet's eyes widened.

He sighed. "I have the devil's own temper, Harriet."

Harriet. He had used her given name. A little thrill shot through her, but that was nothing to the sensation that rippled her spine as he took her hands and regarded her from bottomless pools of dark sensuality.

"I could not abide the notion that you were so free with your favors, that what we shared that afternoon in the meadow—however fleeting—meant nothing. It enraged me."

"But I did not—"

"Hush." He put his finger to her lips. "Later, I realized that you had better taste than to cavort with Oliver Hunt in the shrubbery. Indeed," he murmured, tracing the outline of her mouth with his fingertip, "I find your taste exquisite."

He brushed her lips with his.

"Orange blossoms." He inhaled deeply. "Delightful, but you are wildflowers, Harriet. Wild and free and devoid of guile. I realize that now."

"You d-do?" A strange drumbeat had begun within her, as if her pulse had taken on a new, urgent rhythm.

"What I do not know is what I am going to do about it. It took courage to come here, but it also took something else." He leveled a gaze at her. "I wonder—do you feel anything for me? Am I anything to you other than Freddy's former business partner, the man you have cajoled into this humbling masquerade?"

Harriet tried to understand what he was asking. She took a deep breath. "I . . . I have a regard for you, my lord. You have been very accommodating."

"Regard? Accommodating?" A muscle tightened in his jaw. "I . . . suppose we might build on that." But he sounded dubious.

And then he kissed her. It was a gentle, subdued kiss that carried overtones of regret. Only their lips touched; his hands remained at his sides. Harriet stood motionless, respecting the distance his troubled mood set between them. But his tenderness caught at her soul, and she could not stop her hands from stealing to his waistcoat.

She knew the moment his melancholy gave way to something less definable, for his air of detachment vanished. The space between them narrowed. His kiss grew more insistent, and a sense of urgency swept her. Suddenly, Harriet wanted more, much more, than his kiss.

And then it was as if they were back in that secluded meadow, kissing with abandon amid the clover. His mouth seared hers, then traced a heated path down her neck. His hands were on her waist, her hips, nestling her between his thighs as he pressed her against the desk. Crushed between his solid chest and the unforgiving oak, Harriet gave a breathless, frustrated sigh.

With one motion, he lifted her onto the desk. Now her gaze was at his level, but only for a moment, for he bent to kiss her breast. Heat rose within her as she felt the warmth of his mouth through the fabric of her gown and gave a low, incoherent moan.

Something fell to the floor, something small and insignificant. The sound penetrated the sensual fog that engulfed her, and Harriet suddenly realized that it was not insignificant at all. It was her peace offering, her special creation for him. It was the best of her. He must have it.

"The napoleon!" she cried, scooting off the desk to rescue the little pastry, which had fallen onto the rug. The top crust had split. Cream filling oozed out from the sides.

He stared at her in disbelief. His eyelids were heavy with desire, made more potent by a brooding anger. "Is a damned dessert the only thing that moves you?"

Harriet cradled the napoleon. "No, my lord. Only taste it, please."

She held it out to him. He did not understand, she knew. He would refuse. Helpless sorrow swamped her. It was impossible to explain how important it was that he accept her gift.

Suddenly, he ripped the napoleon from her hands and resentfully bit off a piece.

"Excellent," he snarled. "But what does that matter? Everything you turn your hand to is exquisite."

A bit of the cream filling clung to his cheek. Harriet reached out to wipe it away, but somehow her arms came around his neck instead. He stiffened.

Impulsively, she flicked out her tongue and licked the filling from his skin. It tasted all the more delicious for the fact that it had been part of him, however briefly. Cream and sandalwood and something entirely masculine wreaked havoc with her senses. Harriet sighed in longing.

A shudder racked his body, but he held himself rigid, like a soldier at attention. Under thunderous brows, his gaze grew stormy.

In for a penny, in for a pound, Harriet thought wildly. She took the napoleon from his hand and slowly raised it to his mouth. As his turbulent gaze locked with hers, uncertainty flickered in his eyes.

Harriet touched the napoleon to his lips. They parted involuntarily. Harriet held the pastry from him long enough to capture a bit of the filling on her fingertip and touch it to her own lips. Then, with the same finger, she traced the path along her neck that his kisses had forged moments ago. In its wake, small bits of cream clung to her skin.

With a low, animal like growl, Lord Westwood took her mouth in a quick, bruising kiss. Harriet's fingers went limp, and the napoleon fell to the floor once more, but this time she did not care. Abruptly, he severed the kiss and began to nibble his way along the trail of cream filling that marked her flesh. His tongue seared a path of delicious heat from her neck to her shoulders. Harriet closed her eyes in an agony of desire as he consumed her, bite by bite until at last he brought their lips together again in a fierce kiss.

"I want you. Now." His clipped tone brooked no compromise. His fingers burrowed under her bodice, freeing her breasts for his touch. Harriet almost cried aloud as pleasure ripped through her. She wanted him, too, and she shut her mind to the internal voice that warned of danger and regret. The thing between them, whatever it was, eviscerated her defenses. It made her forget everything except for the pursuit of a joy she had never experienced.

For this short afternoon, she would not be strong. She would be weak—wonderfully, deliciously weak.

Impatiently, his hands roamed over her, creating rivers

of desire deep in her belly. He fumbled with her skirts, pushing them up and out of the way. When his palm grazed her thigh, Harriet gasped in wonder. Her entire world was contained in his touch.

At first she ignored the intrusive scraping sound. Then came the inescapable realization that something was terribly, mortifyingly amiss. The sound had been the door opening. And the curse that came from the direction of the doorway was unmistakable.

"Damn that I should live to see this!"

Harriet's eyes flew open. Over Lord Westwood's shoulder she saw a man moving toward them, brandishing a cane he obviously intended to apply to Lord Westwood's broad back.

"Father!"

Lord Westwood turned. A residue of cream clung to his chin. Fumbling frantically with her clothes, Harriet saw to her horror that a glob of filling sat on the tip of her exposed breast.

"His Grace, the Duke of Sidenham," Lord Westwood's servant intoned just as Harriet's father brought his cane down upon them.

Monica gaped at the crowd of people who traipsed through the door of Harriet's house. First came Harriet, followed by the Duke of Sidenham and a bevy of servants. Eustace, returning from an afternoon ride in the park, looked very confused as he wandered in after them.

"Start packing!" the duke roared. "We leave within the quarter hour." He marched out into the street, where his enormous carriage and two other coaches stood waiting.

The command launched a flurry of activity. Servants scurried here and there, flinging things into boxes. They ignored Harriet's own protesting servants.

"No, you don't!" cried Heavenly, grasping for a maid who carried an armful of Harriet's gowns. Celestial grabbed at another servant, but the man shrugged her off, causing her to tumble to the floor. An irate Horace launched himself to Celestial's rescue and planted the man a facer.

The women's shrieks filled the foyer as the two men pummeled each other in earnest. The maid gave a little cry and darted back up the stairs.

"Stop it!" Harriet cried, horrified at the violent chaos in her foyer. "Stop it this instant!"

"Oh, dear. Oh, dear," murmured Monica, wringing her hands.

The brawling servants crashed into a table, toppling a vase, which Eustace caught and tucked under one arm. He put the other arm protectively around Monica.

"What the devil is going on here!" boomed the duke. He stood in the doorway again, impatience written on his craggy features.

Harriet had seen her father only twice since her marriage to Freddy. His appearance had changed very little. Thick, almost white hair crowned his high, regal forehead. His brows nearly met over his nose, giving him a satyric air. He was not as tall as she remembered, age having given him a slightly stooped appearance. But the arrogance he exuded left no doubt that he was master in every way. All activity in the foyer immediately came to a halt.

"What are you about, Father?" Harriet demanded. "You cannot come here and throw my house and servants into disarray like this. I demand an explanation."

"Demand, do you?" He regarded her coldly. "Very well, Harriet. Alarming news reached me in Cornwall. Your Mr. Stevens neglected to make his usual report to my solicitor in a timely fashion. When my man investigated, he discovered that your solicitor's duties have been taken over by one Jeremy Wilson."

Harriet frowned. "I do not know a Mr. Jeremy Wilson."

"Further, Stevens's handling of your business affairs

shows some irregularities. I come all the way from Cornwall to set matters straight, only to discover that you are off visiting an unmarried man in his home, alone. I dash off to rescue you from such a disgraceful lapse of respectability and find you engaged in lascivious—not to say bizarre—activity with the scapegrace."

Harriet flushed. "It is not what you think."

"No?" The duke drew himself up. "I may be advanced in years, but I am not a complete fool. You have disgraced yourself, daughter. You have neither the means nor the morals to control your behavior. Therefore, I am taking you to my home."

Stunned, Harriet stared at him. "I am my own woman now. I am a widow, no longer under your protection."

"You have made a mess of things. I thought that marriage would improve you, but I was wrong. Since you have always wished to go your own way, I did everything I could to assure your financial independence and freedom. But it seems that I have been hoist by my own petard. You have had too much freedom. Now it is at an end. You will come with me."

"I will not."

Her father merely turned to the assemblage. "A quarter hour," he warned coldly, then vanished from the doorway. Immediately, the servants resumed the packing and carting of boxes as Heavenly, Celestial, and Horace looked on in dismay. Harriet could only stand helplessly as her household was taken apart.

"You did not tell him about the engagement," Monica whispered. "Surely, he would have made allowances for your, er, activities if he had known the earl was your betrothed."

Harriet shook her head. "He would have made us marry immediately. That would not be fair to Lord Westwood."

"Would marriage to him be so terrible?" Monica prodded. "Perhaps your heart is more engaged than you allow."

"No."

"Do not make the mistake that I did," Monica warned. "I have lived my life alone because one man played me false, but not all men are like Francis and Freddy, Harriet. Please give Lord Westwood a chance."

Harriet thought of the tenderness in his eyes, the way his lips had felt on hers—sweet and fierce and beyond anything she had ever imagined. Monica would have her take the chance that he could love her. She almost had. Harriet knew she ought to be grateful to her father for interrupting them before she had given herself completely, irrevocably. She had almost made the worst mistake of her life. Second worst, she amended, after her marriage.

"No," Harriet said firmly. "No."

In a few minutes, her father returned to lead her to his carriage. This time, she did not utter a word of protest.

"I'm not going to let Lady Harriet face her father alone," Heavenly cried. She darted out the front door and wedged her way into the baggage coach containing the very female servant she had earlier assaulted. Slowly, the caravan of carriages pulled away from the house.

Monica shook her head in dismay.

"Do not worry, Mother," Eustace said. "Lady Harriet will right herself. She just needs time to sort it all out."

She eyed him fondly. Her son, it seemed, had acquired some wisdom beyond his years. "Perhaps you are right. Harriet is merely confused at the moment. We have Lord Westwood to thank for that. I hope he knows what he has done."

"If you had seen him floor Hunt the other night, you would have no doubt that he cares for her." Eustace's eyes gleamed.

"Then he needs to do more than sit in his house and ignore her, as he has done for the last two days," Monica groused, although it had not escaped her attention that Eustace's revered Mr. Hunt was now merely "Hunt." If Lord Westwood had accomplished that transformation, she should be grateful. "Perhaps the earl needs to get off his—"

"I am at your service, Mrs. Tanksley."

Monica nearly jumped out of the chair into which she had collapsed after the duke's entourage departed. "Lord Westwood!" The earl stood in the foyer, his expression grim.

"Where has he taken her?" he demanded.

"See?" Eustace beamed. "I knew he would come."

Monica regarded the earl reproachfully. "You are a bit late, my lord. You missed quite a dust-up."

He glowered. "I ask you again, Mrs. Tanksley. Where has that curmudgeon taken Lady Harriet?"

"His home. Wherever that is."

"He mentioned Cornwall," Eustace said helpfully.

"Cornwall?" Monica frowned, thinking hard. "Yes, I seem to remember Harriet once speaking about an estate near Newland."

"Newland! Good God. That is the other end of the country." Lord Westwood whirled and strode toward the door.

"Sir! May I have the honor of accompanying you?" Eustace eyed him hopefully.

Lord Westwood arched a brow. "Should you not stay to assist your mother? She is alone in the house now and will need your protection."

Chastened, Eustace squared his shoulders. "You are right. I had almost forgotten my duty."

"There is no need," Monica began, but at Lord Westwood's warning look, she fell silent. She slanted a gaze at her son. Was it her imagination, or did he stand a little taller after Lord Westwood reminded him of his responsibilities?

"Good luck," she said to the earl and meant it. If any man could make Harriet happy, she sensed it was this one. "If you hurt her, my lord," she added sternly, "I shall not be responsible for the consequences."

But he was already halfway down the steps, dashing to his waiting horse, looking neither right nor left.

And so he collided with the older man who was at that moment approaching Lady Harriet's front steps with a mixture of apprehension and anticipation. The man landed in a heap on the cobblestones.

"Sorry." With a preoccupied expression, Lord Westwood helped him to his feet. When it became apparent that the man was not injured, the earl jumped on his horse and raced away.

Monica put her hand to her mouth. The man Lord Westwood had knocked onto his posterior was none other than Cedric Gibbs. With a deep sense of foreboding, she watched as the squire brushed off his jacket and stared after the horse with a puzzled frown.

Suddenly, his brow cleared. He had finally realized the identity of his inadvertent assailant. A scowl settled over his features. He picked up his hat, shoved it on his head, and climbed the steps.

"Mr. Gibbs!" Monica's heart skipped a beat. Frantically, she looked around, wondering what to do now that Harriet was no longer here to deal with matters.

"Mrs. Tanksley," he acknowledged sourly.

"You have just missed Lord Westwood." She managed a weak smile.

Her remark only deepened his scowl. "Not at all, madam," he said grimly, eyeing the cloud of dust left by Lord Westwood's departing horse. "Not at all."

Monica turned to Eustace. "Is this not wonderful?" she said brightly. "Another houseguest."

Eustace merely regarded his mother as if she had lost her mind.

Chapter Twelve

"Running away again?" Heavenly demanded.

"I do not know what you mean." Harriet looked around the room in which she had lived as a child. The little painted vanity still sat next to the matching cheval glass. The window seat still afforded a marvelous view of the sea. The tall shelves that had held so many of her books still flanked the comfortable feather bed. The room had not changed.

She had changed, however. It seemed incredible that she was back here, a lifetime removed from the lonely child she had been.

"Sure as the fox flees the hound, you are running from Lord Westwood."

Harriet eyed her in amazement. "How can you say that? My father forced me to come."

Heavenly hung one of Harriet's gowns in the wardrobe. "You can tell yourself that if it soothes your conscience."

"There is nothing wrong with my conscience. You were there. He virtually abducted me!"

"Miss Harriet, I've seen you run circles around the likes of Squire Gibbs. I've seen you dash out to that bakery before the chickens were up to bake enough bread to fill the countryside. You run that mill and see to the repairs without so much as blinking an eye. You more than hold your own with those swells in London and their outlandish talk." Heavenly looked her up and down. "If it didn't suit you to come here, you wouldn't have."

Harriet sat down on the bed. "I was not running away."

"Missy, you've been running away from men all your days, and that father of yours is partly to blame. But that don't mean you have to keep doing it."

"My father? But—"

"The man lives like a hermit. I don't know what he sees in this drafty castle, but I do know that it is no place for you. I think you know it, too. Why, you married the first man who offered for you just to get away from here."

"I loved Freddy!" Harriet's eyes filled with tears.

Heavenly nodded. "His lordship was a right charming imp, but he didn't know how to love a woman any more than His Grace knew how to raise a daughter after the duchess died." Heavenly scowled. "Him and his castle by the sea. A lonelier place I have never seen. The man let grief eat him alive. He never saw that his coldness was destroying you."

"I do not know why I let you talk to me like this." Harriet buried her head in her hands.

"Somebody's got to." Tears came to Heavenly's eyes. "You've had two cold men in your life, neither one of them capable of giving you what you need. I guess that's why you shriveled up."

"Shriveled up! That is not true!" Stung, Harriet shook her head in denial.

Heavenly shot her a knowing look. "Lord Westwood knows how to warm a woman's heart, even a shriveled-up one, doesn't he?"

"I am nothing to him." Harriet averted her gaze. "And he is nothing to me."

"That's why you ran away, I suppose—because you don't care a fig for him." Heavenly sighed in exasperation. "Don't think you can lie to me, missy. Lord Westwood is everything that Lord Worthington was not, and you know it."

"No," Harriet said fiercely. "No."

"Funny, I never figured you for such a frightened rabbit. I thought that deep down inside, you were a fighter. I guess I was wrong."

"I wish to marry your daughter. Today, if possible."

The Duke of Sidenham gave Elias a long, hard stare. "You are to be commended for coming all this way to do the proper thing after that shocking scene I witnessed," he said grudgingly. "But—"

"What happened in my study has nothing to do with it," Elias said. "Did your daughter not tell you that we were betrothed?" He saw no purpose in admitting that the proposal was a sham.

Surprise swept the duke's craggy features. And although he looked to have a disposition sour enough to curdle milk, something else flickered in the man's eyes. Hope, perhaps? Elias could not be sure. "Why do you want her?" the duke demanded.

Why, indeed. A wife would be damned inconvenient. How could he leave her for months at a time while he sailed the far seas, looking for spices and exotic foods? More important, how could he entrust his heart into the keeping of another woman? Especially since the first woman he gave it to tossed it back without a word of thanks.

Elias knew he was in the throes of a strange madness. Something in Harriet's eccentric, infuriating soul had grabbed him by the throat and would not let go. He was caught, as sure as any pike on the hook, and he would not be satisfied until he had been pulled ashore, seasoned well, and cooked to perfection in Harriet's loving skillet.

"I cannot do without her," Elias confessed.

"That is what Freddy said," the duke snarled, "but he was thinking only of her dowry."

Elias's gaze narrowed. "Freddy was a transparent man. I imagine you saw through him well enough. Is that not why you made certain his assets went to her and set yourself up as trustee?"

The duke's scornful features crumpled. "Harriet wanted her independence. She would not take money from me, no more than the dowry I had set aside for her. I knew that if Freddy died, she would be just as stubborn. I did not want my daughter to be destitute because she married an inveterate gambler. As trustee, I thought I could protect her. It was easy to break the entail—the title itself was meaningless, as Freddy had little of worth. But I knew the shares were valuable. I had you investigated, you see."

Now it was Elias's turn to look surprised.

"I learned that you were a tough, astute businessman," the duke continued, "something of an expert on exotic spices and the like. I myself enjoy good food, but I have had the benefit of my daughter's cooking. Most of England has not. The country was ready to have its palate awakened. I knew you would make a fortune. As long as Freddy held onto those shares, my daughter would be well served."

The fact that his daughter had divested herself of much of the inheritance he had tried to preserve had not yet come to the duke's attention. Elias weighed whether to mention it, but decided otherwise when the duke's gaze filled with pain.

"She wanted so badly to leave home," he rasped. "It was my fault. I am not an easy man to live with. Her mother died years ago, and she has known no feminine influence besides that absurdly named servant . . ." He frowned.

"Heavenly," Elias supplied.

"What? Oh, yes." The duke took a deep breath. "I am something of a hermit, Westwood. I prefer my solitary state, but Harriet needs people and life. I could not give her that. I suppose that is why she spent all her time in the kitchen. One day I looked up and she had become a woman—like her mother."

The duke was miles away, lost in the past. Elias waited. "I realized I had to do something," the duke said after a time. "Against my better judgment, I took her to London for a Season. She met Freddy, and that was that. She had no experience of men. She did not recognize what he was. I knew that if I forbade the marriage, she would defy me. Harriet can be quite stubborn."

"Yes." Elias tried to imagine Harriet, six years younger and achingly vulnerable, swept into Freddy's aura without the protective armor she had spent subsequent years devising. He saw a father who wanted desperately to assure her happiness, but did not know how.

"I thought I could protect her within the marriage."

"And so you did."

"No, I failed." The duke's brow darkened. "I had him watched. He kept mistresses all over town. I safeguarded her money, but I could do nothing about her heart."

Then the duke leveled an assessing gaze at Elias. "I will not betray her," Elias said, reading the dark intensity in those tormented eyes.

"I thought I was doing what was best," the duke said fiercely. "Instead, I abandoned my parental responsibility. I should have forbade the marriage and taken her off somewhere. Because I did not, she was hurt more deeply than I can imagine. More deeply than she understands." He paused. "I will kill you if you hurt her."

"Do I take that as permission to proceed?" Elias asked with a wry smile.

The duke's heavy sigh encompassed a lifetime of regret. "The only permission you need at the moment," he said softly, "is Harriet's."

* * *

Elias waited impatiently in the duke's drawing room. No wonder Harriet had wanted to leave this place. Perched on the edge of the wild Cornish seas, her father's castle was picturesque but as desolate as the duke himself. This was no place for a woman of Harriet's spirit and warmth. Freddy's winsome ways and charming smile must have made him a godsend to the lonely girl she had been.

But she was a woman now, entirely capable of making up her own mind and not inclined to see any man as a godsend. What if she would not have him?

"Good afternoon, Lord Westwood." She entered the room and moved to stand guardedly beside an upholstered chair. Her plain blue morning dress brought out the dazzling sapphire of her wary, unsmiling eyes.

Elias took a deep breath. "I will come right to the point, Lady Harriet."

"Before . . . in London, you called me Harriet."

For days he had thought of her as Harriet, but a man about to make a marriage proposal took nothing for granted. He cleared his throat. "I beg your pardon."

"Do not. I liked it." She gave him a little half smile, but caution still lurked in her gaze.

"Will you do me the great honor," Elias said distinctly, "of becoming my bride?"

She gasped. Her hand shot out to the chair for support. Damn! He had been too precipitous. He was used to dealing with men, to making himself understood in an efficient, forthright manner. He did not know the flowery things one must say to the woman one wished to marry.

"I should not have spoken so abruptly," he said quickly, feeling like a tongue-tied youth.

She took a little step toward him. "Do not apologize,

my lord. It is just that I was not expecting a proposal of marriage. We agreed to end our engagement in August. I did not think you wished for . . . for another outcome."

"Well, I do wish it, damn it all. It is all that I have wished for since you left me standing in my study with cream all over my face."

Her face flushed scarlet. "Lust is not a reason to marry."

"There is more to it than that, Harriet. Much more."

Shaken, she turned away. "This is very sudden."

Elias placed his hands on her trembling shoulders. "Look at me, Harriet. I would not lie to you. I want nothing more than to spend the rest of my life with you."

"You wish to reform me. I could never marry a man intent on changing me." She shook off his hands.

"What are you talking about?"

"You do not like my salons. You have no use for my cooking—"

"I have every use for your cooking," he protested. "There is no more fervent admirer of your culinary skills than I."

"My bread—"

"Is wonderful, damn it all!" Elias barked, baffled as to why the conversation had suddenly taken this turn.

"Stop it!" she cried. "Bread, sir, is not just flour and leavening—it symbolizes the very essence of life. People must have a little leavening, my lord, or they turn into fossils." Desperation filled her voice. "Change, tolerance, fair-mindedness—these are the things that make life worth living. I cannot modify my beliefs for you. I am my own person. I cannot subsume myself in my husband."

"The way you did with Freddy?"

She gasped. "I never—"

"Yes, by heavens, you did!" Elias thundered. "All this prattle about open-mindedness and tolerance is so much poppycock. Freddy was a liar and a cheat. He was unfaithful from the moment he gave you his name. You tolerated his infidelities—not because you thought it made you a better person—but because you were afraid not to. You buried your pain under all that talk about bread and tolerance in the hope it would go away. But it did not go away, did it Harriet? Underneath it all, it hurt like hell."

"How dare you!" Fury filled her eyes.

Elias's own temper was shot. "Listen to me" he commanded through gritted teeth. "You did not drive Freddy to his death. He would have been untrue to any woman he married. He was incapable of anything else. There was nothing about you, no flaw or inadequacies, that drove him into Caroline Forth's arms."

"You have seen Caroline," she bit out. "She is much more than I could ever be. Beautiful and seductive and—"

"She is a fraud," Elias snapped. "There is not one smattering of genuine feeling in her. She cannot hold a candle to you."

Harriet shook her head in denial. Tears shimmered in her eyes. Elias could stand it no longer. "Damn it, Harriet, you ought to have thrown the bounder out. A person cannot always be tolerant. Sometimes in life a man—or woman—has to take a stand or risk doing irreparable harm. You cannot let fear get in the way."

"Fear?" She brought her chin up defiantly. "I am not afraid, my lord." But her voice quavered.

Again Elias put his hands on her shoulders, this time to give her a little shake. "You are afraid to let yourself care for me. You are afraid I might hurt you—as Freddy did."

The tears that had threatened suddenly spilled onto her cheeks. Elias felt like a cad.

"Harriet," he murmured, pulling her into his arms. "This was not how I meant it to go. I meant to get down on my knees and do it properly, but my temper got the best of me. I simply cannot stand the thought of your being married to Freddy all those years, enduring the pain of his betrayal. I would never betray you, Harriet. Never."

She stood quietly in the circle of his arms, but she held herself stiffly, withholding herself. Elias had no choice but to release her.

"I will think about your offer, my lord," she said quietly. And she left him.

Elias swore softly.

"This is better news than I could have hoped for," Jeremy Wilson said proudly.

Henry slumped in the hard wooden chair in Wilson's office. He had left a damned good bottle of wine to respond to the solicitor's urgent summons.

"I never thought to have such success, but even that Hunt fellow finally agreed to our terms. Not graciously, but he agreed nevertheless—especially after I explained that Lord Westwood might feel compelled to present his offer in person. Scared him to death, it did. Henry, you may go and inform his lordship that I have successfully repurchased all of the shares Lady Harriet sold."

Henry frowned. "The earl is in Cornwall." He had tried all week not to think about the import of Lord Westwood's hasty trip to Cornwall. He had never seen the earl go to such extremes over a woman.

The solicitor nodded. "That is why I have summoned you. You are Lord Westwood's most trusted aide. I know I can count on you to deliver the news to him personally."

"What? To Cornwall?" Henry eyed him in disbelief. " 'Tis a three-day ride! And deuced uncomfortable, too. Three days in the saddle, dashing over hill and dale just to have the earl sing Jeremy Wilson's praises while fine wine sat awasting in London. "I won't do it."

The solicitor's gaze narrowed. "I know you like your comforts, Henry. And I know you live quite well when Lord Westwood is away. But the earl has made this bit of business his highest priority. He would not look kindly on your refusal to cooperate."

Henry sighed. Wilson had spoken the truth. He had no desire to risk the earl's temper. Scowling, he scraped back his chair. "Very well. Give me the papers."

Cornwall. Godforsaken Cornwall.

"Mrs. Tanksley?"

Monica looked up from her knitting. Squire Gibbs sat on the edge of his chair, glowering at the corner of the room where Eustace sat reading a book.

"Yes, Mr. Gibbs?"

"How long must I stay in this house?"

Her spirits sank. She had found the week with Squire Gibbs most companionable. As she had long suspected, he was not the ogre some people thought. Indeed, he seemed to be a changed man since she had last seen him in Sussex. He had shed some weight, and his face had lost its florid appearance. Since his arrival in London, he had had little to drink, with the result that their evenings had been spent in pleasant conversation, their days in quiet walks. She had assumed that he, too, enjoyed their time together. Now she realized that her loneliness had led her to see friendship where there was only tolerance.

"Until Harriet returns, I suppose," she replied quietly. "She is eager to speak to you about the job."

"If she is so eager, why isn't she here?" he growled.

Monica bit her lip. "I did not realize that passing time in my company was such an onerous chore." Oh, dear, why had she said that?

Surprise swept his features. "It is not," he quickly assured her. "It is just that, well—" He broke off.

Monica placed her knitting in her lap. "Yes?" she prodded warily.

"That son of yours."

"Eustace? What about him?"

"He has appointed himself your chaperone." He reddened.

Monica had noticed that Eustace rarely left her alone with Mr. Gibbs. Her son was taking his new responsibilities as head of the household very seriously. The knowledge that Mr. Gibbs found Eustace's watchfulness irritating cheered her. Perhaps he was not completely indifferent to her after all. "Does that bother you, sir?" she asked carefully.

He looked away. "I am not a man to spend my days in inaction. There are things to be done in Sussex. If the mill is to be properly fitted for the milling season, certain steps have to be taken."

"Then you mean to accept Lady Harriet's job offer?" Monica asked, surprised.

"Lady Harriet has been most generous," he said stiffly, "especially given the way I have treated her. It has taken me a while to realize that."

Monica absorbed his words in stunned silence. "What steps, Mr. Gibbs?" she finally ventured, willing him to look at her.

Abruptly, he did. She was startled to realize how very blue were his eyes. "What's that, Mrs. Tanksley?"

"What steps must be taken before the mill can be fitted for the milling season?" Bluer than the sea, she decided.

"The chute has to be oiled, the hopper cleaned, and I am convinced that the angle of the shoe is all wrong. Those Essex designers don't know a thing about Sussex wheat." He hesitated. "Surely, this does not interest you."

"On the contrary, Mr. Gibbs." Monica gave him an encouraging look. "I am riveted."

Cedric beamed. "What most excites me is the possibility of obtaining black lava stone."

"Lava stone?"

"From Coblenz, on the Rhine. More accessible, now that the war is over. Lava rock makes the hardest millstones, and it can be cut and grooved with great precision. An experienced miller can set the stones very close together, so that the meal could be ground very fine. Lady Harriet would have the whitest, smoothest flour for miles around!" He said this with such excitement that Monica smiled.

"Why, Mr. Gibbs, I do believe you are quite determined."

He regarded her somberly. "I keep thinking about my children and what might happen if I could not provide for them. Without the mill, I don't mind telling you that our income has been drastically depleted. Lady Harriet has offered me a way out, and I believe I must take it."

"I do hope your children have not suffered." Monica was troubled. She had assumed Mr. Gibbs's finances were not what they were during the years his family controlled the mill, but she did not know his situation was dire.

"Only from the lack of a woman's influence," he said. "We are not destitute, but I have been feeling quite a fool these days. I should be shot for thinking that Lady Harriet—or any woman—would have the likes of me." He shook his head. "I have been very selfish."

Their gazes held. Monica's insides began to tremble as her heart filled with longing and foolish hope. But perhaps it was not so foolish after all, for he was studying her with a very odd expression. Indeed, his eyes held something very like the hope that echoed in her own heart.

Monica glanced over at her son, who was trying not to appear to eavesdrop. "Eustace?" she called.

He rose, ready to do battle for his mother's honor. "Yes, Mother?" He glowered at the squire.

"I promised Mrs. Thornton that I would return this book to her." Monica took a book from the table near her chair. "She lent it to me more than two weeks ago."

"Mrs. Thornton? Heavenly's friend in Kensington?" Eustace frowned. "Very well. I will return it tomorrow."

"She is a shut-in, Eustace. She does not sleep well. I would prefer that you take it tonight. I would not have her sleeplessness on my conscience."

He eyed her incredulously. "But it is eight o'clock. It will be nine before I can get there—if I remember the way. Can this errand not wait until—"

"Tonight," Monica said firmly. "If you please."

"But—" He broke off. His gaze darted from his mother to Squire Gibbs, who was regarding him steadily. Eustace glared at the book in his mother's hand. Then, without a word, he took it and strode from the room.

"I believe that boy is growing up," Cedric said carefully.

"Not a moment too soon," Monica replied, trying to sound cheerful, though she felt a bit nervous now that they were alone. "Would you care for a brandy?"

"I'm not one for spirits these days."

"You are to be commended for your self-discipline, Mr. Gibbs."

Cedric did not immediately reply. Instead, he eyed her thoughtfully. "Mrs. Tanksley?"

"Yes?" To her great embarrassment, the word came out a squeak.

"We have known each other for many years. And yet, I feel as though I am seeing you for the first time. Do you understand what I mean?"

Monica's heart turned a little somersault. "I think s-so," she stammered.

"Then I hope you will understand when I say that I hope Eustace gets quite lost in Kensington." Rising, he reached for her hand.

"Oh, dear," Monica said breathlessly as she realized his intent. "Oh, dear, oh, dear."

"My sentiments exactly," he murmured, and pulled her into his arms.

Chapter Thirteen

Elias knew that rage came in many forms. Hot anger could turn a man into an instant fool and blind him to all reason. But sometimes rage actually sharpened reason, elevating it to the deadly keenness of a newly honed stiletto. Zephyr's abandonment on their wedding day had produced something close to that. And while Elias had gotten over that debacle, he would never get over Harriet's stiff, dispassionate reception of his proposal.

I will think about your offer, my lord. The words conveyed no joy, no hope. She meant to reject him.

But she had figured without his rage—not blind, irrational anger, but the cold, calculating fury that throughout history had spawned brilliant schemes of revenge, murder, abduction.

Sweet, satisfying abduction.

Elias dismounted, careful to stay within the shadows of the castle. He patted the special license in his pocket. She would learn that he was not to be denied. He had never lost a battle—in war or business. And he feared nothing.

Except losing her.

What a nitwit he had been! Telling himself he wanted only his shares, when in truth he wanted only her. Harriet made him forget Zephyr Payne and Caroline Forth and any number of women in between. Harriet had mesmerized him from that first morning in the bakery. Even then, though her stubborn independence infuriated him, he had desired her.

But it was not just desire between them. It was primrose and napoleons and those strange, fermenting cultures and the awful salons she chose to fill with rabble-rousing idiots. It was all of that and more, and for the first time since looking up from a hospital bed into Zephyr's lovely face, Elias knew himself enslaved.

He had to marry Harriet, to claim her for all time. He could not rest until he had her.

Sooner or later, perhaps, she would understand how she had allowed Freddy's behavior to blind her to her own worth. Perhaps she would even see why her father, though well-meaning, had abandoned her when she most needed his protection against Freddy's charm. But by the time Harriet realized those things, Elias suspected he would be an old man. If he hoped to marry her now, he would have to force her to the altar and risk destroying whatever affection she held for him.

It was a breathtaking risk. But a man who risked nothing had nothing.

All was in readiness. Elias had taken a room at the Pig and Whistle Inn, about an hour's ride from the duke's seaside castle. He was determined that Harriet would pass the night in his company. He knew that Sidenham would then force her to marry him, regardless of her wishes.

The only unsettled details concerned the actual abduction itself. Harriet's room was on an upper floor of the castle. From the ground he could see the window seat from which she looked out over the churning seas. The view must be magnificent, but lonely as a tomb. In his travels Elias had seen magnificent sights men would kill to behold, but every one of nature's marvels had cried out for a companion to witness their beauty. The image of Harriet as a lonely young girl, perched in that window and watching the sea thrash endlessly against the cliffs, brought a lump to his throat.

Ruthlessly, he banished sentiment and stared at the castle wall. More than a hundred feet of smooth, sheer stone lay between the ground and that window. Sidenham's castle must have been damned near impregnable to generations of invaders—even to invaders of the heart.

It would help if he had a confederate in that fortress, but speed, daring, and surprise were on his side. They would have to serve.

His horse neighed quietly as Elias tied it to a branch in a copse of trees at the edge of the castle wood. The clear afternoon had given way to dusk and rolling fog.

Fog and darkness. Perfect cover for a man bent on abduction—he hoped.

Heavenly was carrying a dinner tray to Harriet's room, which she had not left since Lord Westwood's unexpected visit a few days ago. She sat for hours at her window, listless and sad, giving her meals only an indifferent glance. Heavenly worried, for if there was anything Harriet took an interest in, it was food. Though Harriet had not shared the details of her private meeting with the earl, Heavenly knew he was the cause of her mistress's distress.

And so, when Heavenly saw Lord Westwood standing in the great hall, demanding that the hapless footman produce Lady Harriet forthwith, Heavenly shot over to him.

"How dare you bother my Harriet!" she demanded furiously. "Haven't you done enough to the poor lass?"

Lord Westwood's icy gaze shifted from the unhappy footman to her. "You would be Heavenly, I presume."

"*Miss* Heavenly to you, and to anyone who hurts my baby," she huffed.

To her surprise, his lips curled into a half smile. "I see

you have your mistress's welfare at heart. I gather she is not entirely happy at the moment?"

"Happy! As if she has known the meaning of the word since you wormed your way into her life."

But for all her bluster, Heavenly had been covertly studying his lordship's steely gaze. Almost, she believed this man could save her poor, shriveled-up dear. Almost, she believed his strength of will could overcome the barriers Harriet had erected between herself and happiness.

Suddenly, and to the footman's amazement, Heavenly took Lord Westwood's arm and pulled him aside. "What are you really doing here, my lord?" she asked softly. "What do you want?"

"Harriet," he ground out. "I will not leave without her."

I will not leave without her. Could it be? A love that would be true, enduring, faithful? Heavenly glared at him even as joy surged within her. "I'll not be party to anything that hurts her," she warned.

"Nor will I. And now, *Miss* Heavenly," he said, his voice deadly calm, "either get out of my way, or take me to her. One way or the other, I mean to have her."

And so you shall. With a silent prayer of thanksgiving, Heavenly shoved the dinner tray into his hands. "Follow me," she said grimly.

Harriet did not look up when Heavenly brought in the tray. The last thing she wanted was another bowl of Cook's beef knuckle soup, which would have been helped enormously by a pinch of tarragon.

"Close the door, Heavenly," she said crossly, staring out into the gathering fog. "You are letting in the draft."

Harriet felt, rather than heard, the door swing shut. That in itself was unusual, for Heavenly had been slamming doors for several days to show her displeasure at

Harriet's refusal to unburden herself of her private thoughts. Perhaps she was trying a different tactic.

"It is no use, dear." Harriet sighed. "I have nothing to say about Lord Westwood. And were you to ask him, I am sure that he would have nothing to say about me. So let us simply pretend that the man does not exist."

"Too cruel, Harriet," said a masculine voice. "Too cruel."

Harriet jumped from her seat. "My lord!"

He stood in the center of her room—dominated it, in fact. The devil himself could not have looked more dangerous than Lord Westwood did with his flowing cape, beaver hat, and sheathed sword. He eclipsed the little painted vanity, her bookshelves, even her large feather bed. Her entire room became a backdrop for his commanding presence.

"Why are you here?" Harriet managed. Her heart was racing so fast she could scarcely breathe. Where in the world was Heavenly? Had he done something to her? "Why do you have that sword?"

"In the event I have to slay dragons. Get your things."

"What th-things?" Harriet stammered.

"I am taking you away. We will be wed—tonight if you wish, though I see no reason to rouse a cleric from his bed to sanction what he can just as easily sanction tomorrow." His black gaze slammed into hers as he paused to let his words sink in. "Either way, Harriet, tonight is ours."

Harriet made for the door. But he was quicker and caught her in his arms. She suppressed a shriek. The castle walls were too thick to make herself heard, and she did not want him to see her fear. "What have you done with Heavenly?" she demanded with false bravado.

"Nothing," he replied calmly, studying her. "Do you think me a monster, Harriet? I promise you, I am not."

Temper or no, he would never hurt a woman. Somehow she knew that. There could be only one answer to her question. "Heavenly! *She* brought you up here!"

"What does it matter?" Without warning, he swept her off her feet and into his arms. "We can leave quietly, without alerting the entire castle, or you can make a fuss. But make no mistake, Harriet—you leave with me." His granite-hard eyes darkened, underscoring his intent.

"My father." Harriet brightened. "He will never allow—"

"Your father is otherwise engaged." He carried her to the door. "Heavenly is most resourceful."

"Stop this!" Tears welled in her eyes. "I am not a sack of potatoes to be carted here and there by you or my father or whatever man requires my presence. I am my own person. I *am*!"

"No," he agreed, "you are not a sack of potatoes."

"I hate you!" she bit out as he opened the door.

"Harriet." His expression grew grave.

Sniffing, she wiped her eyes with her sleeve. "What?"

"If I thought that was true I would leave you here. But it is not true, is it?"

Harriet could not speak. Her heart fluttered wildly. He held her so close she could feel the pounding of his heart. His breathing seemed to stop as he stared at her intently.

Mutely, she shook her head. He expelled a sharp breath. And then the world started to move again as he carried her from the room.

In the end, it had been amazingly easy. Elias carried Harriet down two long, circular stairways, past her father's study, and through the great hall without incident. One or two servants stopped to stare, but they did not attempt to intervene. Heavenly obviously had matters well in hand. When the obstreperous footman who had tried to prevent Elias from entering the castle watched calmly as he strode off with the duke's daughter, Elias's estimation of Heavenly's skills soared. If only he had managers like her at Westwood Imports.

Harriet remained silent as he carried her out to his waiting mount and tossed her on the horse's back like . . . like a sack of potatoes. She held herself stiffly, looking anywhere but at him.

As he set the horse toward the inn, Elias wondered what thoughts were racing through her brain. Now that the first flush of success was over, now that he had pulled off the impossible and snatched Harriet from her father's fortress, the long night stretched out before him, its resolution by no means certain.

She could have stopped him. She could have looked him in the eye and said she cared nothing for him, and he would have left her there with her feather bed and cold soup. But she had not stopped him.

And now what? How would he turn her silent acquiescence into something much, much more?

Harriet surveyed the private parlor. It was clean and comfortable-looking, and the meal waiting on the table smelled better than anything Cook had produced.

But she was alone with Lord Westwood. Utterly alone. He intended for them to spend the night in this cozy inn, miles from her father's home. And though it had seemed almost natural to put her hands around his middle and ride off into the night, now she could scarcely meet his gaze. She felt confused, awkward, angry. How dare he invade her home and carry her off?

As she contemplated the dressed mutton chops before them, however, her anger began to fade. She had not eaten a decent meal in days, and the heady aroma of well-seasoned mutton was most persuasive. With a resigned sigh, Harriet sat in the chair that Lord Westwood had been patiently holding for her.

"A wise decision," he murmured. "Mrs. Melbourne is

said to be famous for her mutton chops. Perhaps she will even give you the recipe."

Harriet glared as he seated himself. Spearing a piece of mutton with her fork, she lifted her chin defiantly. They ate in silence, the air between them thick with tension. After a bit, Lord Westwood refilled her glass. The wine was excellent. Though it bore no label, it had to be the product of the smuggling trade that flourished on Cornish shores. Her appreciation of the wine did not escape him.

"The French ever did understand the grape, do you not agree?" he said idly.

Of course Lord Westwood's discriminating nose would not miss a fine French wine. That he could so casually comment upon it—as if sharing an intimate meal in an isolated inn was perfectly ordinary—infuriated her.

"Where do you think this vintage is from, my lord?" Harriet asked in a resentful, sardonic tone. "Bordeaux, perhaps? The northern coast? I am sure that as a man of such discerning tastes, you must be dying to tell me."

"Neither," he said, seemingly oblivious to her fury. "It is more substantial than a Bordeaux, but fruitier than the coastland vintages. An inland wine, I think. Strong and lusty, with a hint of the oak that aged it." He gave her a little salute with his glass and took another sip of wine.

Let him ramble on, Harriet thought. Now that she had food in her stomach, her mind was beginning to rouse itself. She had to escape. Perhaps she could throw herself on the mercy of Mrs. Melbourne. No, that would not work—Lord Westwood had probably paid the woman well, which accounted for the fine wine at their table.

Perhaps she could slip away on the pretext of refreshing herself, and make off with his horse. Or perhaps . . .

"Trust," he said suddenly.

"I . . . what?" Harriet stared at him.

"Trust. Imperative between partners, business or otherwise. That is your problem, Harriet. You have not learned to trust me."

She eyed him in frosty disdain. "I cannot imagine why I would trust a man who will do anything to get his precious shares—even lower himself to pretend to be my fiancé. Or," she added pointedly, "abduct me."

"No reason," he agreed.

"Or seduce me to make sure I cooperated."

"I never tried to seduce you."

She eyed him incredulously. "What occurred in your study is ample proof, sir. Had not my father arrived, you would have—" She broke off, embarrassed.

"Taken you right there on the desk." There was no hint of apology in his tone. "But you would have been safe enough had you not started that business with the pastry. Licking cream from a man's flesh does not convey maidenly reluctance, my dear. A man can stand only so much."

Harriet looked away, remembering her moment of weakness, when she had wanted him more than anything in the world. He touched her chin, forcing her to look at him.

"If it is any consolation," he said softly, "I was utterly miserable pretending to be your fiancé."

"You were?"

"I detest engagements of any kind. If I truly wanted to marry a woman, I would never enter into a formal engagement with her. Too many things can happen."

"Such as?"

"She might leave me standing at the altar in front of the prime minister, the Prince Regent, and three thousand others while she eloped with a titled dandy whose brain was roughly the size of a peacock's." He shot her a rueful smile.

Aghast, Harriet stared at him. "Never say such a thing happened to *you*?"

"It does not matter now. One must move beyond the past. I have done so, and now you must, too."

"I do not know what you mean." But she did.

His gaze narrowed. "Your husband was a cheat, your father a cold fish. No wonder you do not trust the male of the species. We have left you high and dry. Any tender feeling you may have had has been pulverized like those deliciously riced potatoes Mrs. Melbourne made for us."

"I do not wish to speak of this," she retorted in a tight voice.

"You must."

Harriet looked away. "I do not intend to marry you, my lord. I do not intend to marry again, ever. I am an—"

"Independent woman," he finished. "But you need me, Harriet. It is quite all right to acknowledge that."

"You . . . you insufferably conceited man!" Harriet rose. It was time to stop this game of cat and mouse. "I do not know why you think we should suit. We are nothing alike. I will not have you, Lord Westwood, and that is that."

"I am too high-handed?" He rose as well.

"Exactly. You seem to think that because you wish for a thing, it will be handed to you—"

"On a silver salver?" he murmured.

Harriet did not like the way he moved around the table toward her. "You have the arrogance to think you can reform me, when I have no wish to change anything about my life."

"And here I thought change was to be tolerated—nay, sought—at all cost." His hand caught her lightly about the waist. "Is that not what you preach, my dear?"

"You are twisting my words." Harriet flailed ineffectively at his hands. "Stop it, my lord. I vow I cannot think!"

"You were saying that I am arrogant and high-handed and bent on changing you. That I do not have the sense to appreciate you as you are."

His face drew nearer. It was not difficult to read his intent. "Do not kiss me, my lord," Harriet pleaded. "Please do not!"

"And what if I were to say that you are right, Harriet?" he murmured. "That I am all of those things—arrogant and high-handed and manipulative—but that I will not try to change you?"

"Do you not see?" she demanded, exasperated. "You are trying now! You want me to be something that I am not, to do something that I do not wish to do. You want me to . . . to *trust* you, for goodness' sake, when—"

"When you have never trusted a man in your life? Yes, Harriet. I am asking you to do that."

As his mouth descended to hers, Harriet closed her eyes in defeat. His lips were gentle, coaxing, and she could not help but respond. The fury and frustration she felt at his impossible demands and her own inadequacies soon grew into another sort of heat altogether.

He drew her into his arms. And when their hearts pressed against each other, it did not feel like defeat.

"You!"

Henry stared at the angry woman at the door. He was quite sure he had never laid eyes on her before, though she seemed to recognize him. She was not bad-looking, but her glare was sharp enough to kill a man at twenty paces. How fitting that she presided over this frigid old pile of stones. "I am looking for Lord Westwood," he began. "If you will tell me where I might find him—"

"You're the one who brought that note!" She grabbed his arm.

Before Henry could gather his senses, she jerked him inside, pushed him into a little room, and slammed the door shut. Then she rounded on him.

"In London, it was. I recognized you right away. You brought that note round to the kitchen door. The one that said it was from that Hunt fellow. Only it wasn't. You're the one started all the trouble!"

Alarm shot through him. "I do not know a Mr. Hunt," Henry protested, wondering how a wild-eyed harpy in Cornwall came to know of his scheme. "I am in Lord Westwood's employ. I have important business for him."

"His lordship has more important business on his plate at the moment," she snapped. To his horror, she walked over to a desk, pulled out a pistol, and leveled it at him.

"Now," she said, glowering, "suppose you tell me why you wanted Lord Westwood to think Lady Harriet was dallying with Mr. Hunt." As he watched in horror, she cocked the weapon. Henry knew a thing or two about guns. The pistol pointed at his heart was a Manton, known for its hair trigger. He swallowed hard.

"W-w-why?" he echoed.

Slowly, she smiled—the kind of smile a crocodile might give a helpless rat who had the misfortune to wander into its lair.

Chapter Fourteen

Elias slept on the taproom floor.

Despite Harriet's passionate response to his kiss, she did not yet trust him enough to let down her defenses. When he had reined in his rampant desire long enough to study her face for an answer to the question that burned within him, he saw that doubt and denial eclipsed the desire in her eyes. And so, though he had wanted her beyond all wanting, Elias had sent her alone to the little room upstairs he had chosen for their wedding night because it looked over a stream-lined glade instead of the noisy stable yard.

Shrugging into his jacket, Elias tried to ignore his protesting shoulder muscles. He had not slept on a floor in a very long time. Even on the Peninsula, a man could usually scrape together a pallet of straw. But with the inn full, he had had to share the taproom floor with several peddlers, servants who had been turned out of their beds to make room for paying guests, and a farm lad who had drunk too much ale to walk out the front door.

As he climbed the stairs to the room they were to have shared, Elias fought a growing despair. What a fool he had been—playing the dashing hero come to carry his lady off on a fine charger. In truth, he had no idea how to court a woman. Those who wanted him had come willingly. The others had not seemed worth the trouble.

But this maddening widow with her eccentric notions

had enslaved him. The prospect of not having her left an empty feeling in his gut Elias did not care to explore. He only knew that losing her would eat away at him in a way that losing Zephyr Payne had not.

On the stairs he met the maid and persuaded her to give him the breakfast tray she was carrying to Harriet. Standing in the hall, waiting for her to answer his knock, Elias had never felt so foolish. Then the door opened, and his heart jumped to his throat.

"My lord!" Little lines at the corner of her eyes told him she had slept no better than he.

"You need not sound so surprised," he said, more sharply than he intended. "Did you think I would leave you here?"

"No . . . that is, I hoped you would not." Quickly, she took the tray and set it on the table next to the bed. "I trust you slept well?"

Elias moved into the room, trying not to notice that the covers on what would have been his side of the bed remained smooth and untouched. "As well as a bear on a bed of porcupine needles." Resolutely, Elias tore his thoughts away from Harriet's bed. "I have a carriage waiting to take us to London."

She turned away. "Then, we do not . . . wed today?"

"No, but I have a special license in my pocket. Should the spirit move you during our trip, do not hesitate to speak up. Meanwhile, eat something."

She did no more than nibble at a piece of bread as Elias stood stiffly, trying to look at anything besides that delectable mouth. His gaze strayed again to the bed. The inn was no palace, but the room was clean and the bed comfortable-looking. They would have passed a pleasant night under those covers, wrapped in each other's arms.

Pleasant? Elias knew he was deluding himself. A night with Harriet would surpass pleasant. It would surpass his wildest dreams.

Harriet put the piece of bread back on the tray. Their gazes met. Elias cleared his throat. "Are you ready? We had best be on our way before your fath—"

"Too late," came a low growl. The Duke of Sidenham stood grandly at the threshold, his cape flowing out behind him, his crown of white hair radiating authority.

"Father!" Harriet exclaimed.

He strode to her side. "Are you all right, daughter?"

"Of course, but—"

"He did not force himself on you?"

Harriet turned scarlet. "Oh, no. In fact—"

"Good. Else I would have to kill him." The duke regarded Elias with an odd mixture of fury and approval. "I trust you have a special license?"

Nodding, Elias suppressed an urge to give the duke a hearty hug for his fortuitous timing.

"Good," the duke snapped. "Mrs. Melbourne, fetch the vicar."

The innkeeper, who had been standing behind the duke, hastened away. Elias noticed that several people crowded together out in the hall, watching the scene in Harriet's chamber unfold. He did not mind witnesses. They could only help his situation.

"Oh, no, Father!" Harriet protested. "That is not necessary. I am no child. I am a married woman."

"You are a widow," the duke corrected stonily. "And while many of the breed comport themselves in a common fashion, I will not tolerate such behavior in my daughter."

Harriet turned to Elias. "Why do you not say something? Tell him that you slept downstairs, that nothing happened between us. Tell him!"

"It does not matter what did or did not happen," Elias returned calmly. "The perception exists. Your father is right." He stifled a grin. This was so much better than he could have hoped.

A mixture of disbelief and outrage settled over Harriet's features.

Mrs. Melbourne's departure had permitted Heavenly to work her way into the room. "I am sorry, Lord Westwood," she said. "I tried my best to keep His Grace busy, but—"

"By Jove, woman!" the duke thundered, "I will have you flogged. I should have known you were up to something when you set that chess board in front of me last night."

Heavenly seemed unfazed. "He demanded another game, and then a game of all-fours," she told Elias with a shrug. "Starved for company, if you ask me."

The duke made a strangled sound, which Heavenly also ignored. "I was so tired this morning that when that man of yours came round, I let my anger get the best of me. I fired a pistol at him—which I don't regret, except that it roused the duke, who demanded a complete explanation. I had to tell him that you had taken Harriet." She glowered at the man who was edging into the room.

"Thank God she's a miserable shot," Henry put in as he pushed past Heavenly. "But we came in time, didn't we, my lord?"

"Henry?" Elias blinked.

"I heard the lady say that you spent the night downstairs, so everything is all right," Henry continued with a relieved grin. "You don't have to marry her—"

"Of course he has to." Heavenly jabbed Henry's arm. "Just because *you* have the morals of a snake, doesn't mean everyone else does."

"I only meant to save Lord Westwood," Henry protested. "He's not the sort who ought to marry. Has the devil's own temper, you know. I wouldn't swear to the safety of any woman who has to live with a man like that."

"Henry . . ." Elias said warningly.

"So you took it upon yourself to write those notes, pretending to be someone you ain't, stirring up trouble where there wasn't any," Heavenly said in a scathing tone. "You're a liar and a poor specimen of a man to boot."

Elias frowned. "What notes?"

"He wrote one to Miss Harriet pretending to be that fellow Hunt and one to Hunt in her name. He was trying to get them together so that you would be left high and dry. Imagine that!"

"I knew it!" Harriet exclaimed. "Did I not tell you that someone had tricked us, my lord?"

The duke roused himself from contemplation of Heavenly's fate. "What's this?"

Henry ignored the ducal scowl, but his employer's darkening features gave him pause. " 'Twas for your own good, my lord," he insisted. "Marriage is no state for a man accustomed to his freedom. The idea of living in a house with all those women must be abhorrent to you."

Elias studied his longtime batman. "Tell me, Henry, did you by any chance nudge my other fiancée in a similar direction?"

"*Other* fiancée?" The duke looked confused.

Henry shot Elias a lame smile. "You'd be surprised what a note can do to a woman's inclinations. She and that young lord had been making eyes at each other for weeks. You didn't see it, but I noticed it every time I attended you in the hospital. He was in the bed next to yours, if you recall. I sent her only a few letters, begging for a word of tenderness to help heal my—*his*—wounds. She wrote back, and I added a few special words before passing the note on to him, and one thing led to another. As for Hunt, it was easy to discover that he was a frequent visitor to Lady Harriet's salons. Had to have a *tendre* for her. I took it from there," he added proudly.

"*What* other fiancée?" the duke roared.

"Zephyr Payne," Elias explained. "She ran off with another man." He paused. "Thank God."

Henry brightened. He turned to Heavenly. "See? I told you the earl was a right sort. He don't want to wed, and that's the truth."

"No," Elias corrected, "it is not."

Henry frowned. "But, my lord—"

"I will deal with you later," Elias said coolly. "At the moment, I have a wedding to attend."

"But that's what I've been trying to tell you!" Henry exclaimed. "You don't need to marry her. Wilson has bought back the shares she sold!"

Harriet gasped.

"Shares?" the duke repeated, his brow thunderous.

Elias shot a murderous look at his batman. "Go on," he said in a dangerous voice.

"Mr. Wilson summoned me to his office and laid it all out. He was most anxious that you have the news posthaste. The purchasers were happy to sell, since you offered much more than they paid. Even that fellow Hunt finally gave in. So you see, my lord," Henry finished happily, "you have the controlling interest. You don't need her anymore."

"Then again," Harriet interjected in a brittle tone, "why stop with a controlling interest, when you could get all the shares by marrying me?"

Elias leveled his gaze at her. "I am not marrying you to get my hands on those shares."

"Are we speaking about that business of yours, Westwood?" the duke demanded.

Elias nodded. "Your daughter sold off some of her shares to pay for various enterprises. I needed to recover them. It was a business decision, nothing more."

"Business, was it?" Harriet's eyes flashed. "Am I to understand that all between us was merely business?"

"Why in God's name did you sell off the shares?" The duke rounded on his daughter. "As trustee, I gave you complete freedom, but I never expected that you would do such a foolish thing. Why did you not come to me if you needed money?"

"I do not want your money!" Harriet cried. "I never have! All I wanted was your—" She broke off, eyeing him helplessly. Then she ran from the room, sobbing. Glaring at all of them, Heavenly raced after her.

"My . . . what?" The duke shook his head in confusion.

Elias pondered the question. A number of possibilities came to mind, but he did not voice them.

"I gave her everything," the duke insisted, bewildered.

"I know," Elias said sympathetically.

"Women!" Henry spat out.

Elias's brows came together. "As for you—"

"My lord!" called a cheerful female voice. All eyes turned to the doorway, where Mrs. Melbourne stood looking inordinately pleased. She stepped aside to reveal a small man, nervously adjusting his spectacles. He looked as if he had dressed hurriedly, for his clothing was askew and his hair stuck out from his head at odd angles.

"I have brought the vicar," she announced happily. "The wedding can begin!"

Henry groaned. The duke cursed.

Mrs. Melbourne gazed around the room uncertainly. Harriet's absence did not go unnoticed. "Do we have the, er, bride?" she asked delicately.

"Yes," Elias replied calmly. "Somewhere."

Her husband sat opposite her in the carriage. They had barely spoken since the inn, when a vicar Harriet had never met joined them for life before her father, Heavenly, a beaming Mrs. Melbourne, and Lord Westwood's meddling servant—who had looked as unhappy as Harriet.

For three days she and the earl had traveled in silence, neither attempting to bridge the strained gap between them. To Harriet's great relief, the inns at which they stopped had not been full; he had been able to obtain separate rooms.

She did not want to be married to Lord Westwood. She did not want to live with another man who had the power to hurt her. She had hated it when he sought her out before the ceremony and said he would be honored to have her as his wife and deeply regretted she had little choice in the matter. Though he seemed sincere, Harriet suspected he had manipulated everything. Shares and all, she had played right into his hands.

Harriet consoled herself with the knowledge that she would not have to live with him for very long. Soon he would be on his travels again, back to whatever islands held those plantations of his. She might see him no more than once a year. She would continue with her life, and everything would be the same except for the minor inconvenience of having a husband out there somewhere.

No one understood how important it was to have her own things. She loved her salons, where ideas flourished in the stimulating atmosphere of her little town house, and her country estate, where she could make sure that her less fortunate neighbors never wanted for the bread of life.

In her years on this earth, she had accomplished something. She had become a person of worth. No husband—or father, for that matter—could keep her from continuing to do those things. She had made that very clear to Lord Westwood before the wedding ceremony.

"I shall not change for you, my lord," she vowed. "Do not think you can reform me, for you will not."

When he did not reply, she felt bold enough to add, "I

feel no wifely obligations to you and shall exert no wifely claim. You are free to go your own way, and I will go mine."

He had frowned at that, but before he could speak, Mrs. Melbourne had rushed in dithering about the vicar having to preside at a funeral and not being able to wait any longer. At the ceremony, which was blessedly short, Lord Westwood wore a particularly intent expression as the vicar rambled on about wedded bliss.

Wedded bliss—an oxymoron, if ever she heard one.

Her marriage to Lord Westwood would be exactly like her marriage to Freddy. She would learn to tolerate it.

Tolerance was important in all things.

"Celestial! Look at this!" Horace peered out the window at the carriages. Celestial raced to his side.

"Why, 'tis Lady Harriet!" Celestial beamed. "I knew she would find a way around that father of hers. I'd better hurry and get a supper on the table. She will be famished."

Horace put a restraining hand on her arm. "Not so fast. Look, there is Lord Westwood, and he's got his hand on her waist in a, er—" He broke off, momentarily at a loss for words.

"Proprietary manner," Celestial finished, her gaze narrowing. "Do you think they are lovers yet?"

Horace coughed delicately. "It is none of our business. Anyway, how could we tell by looking at them?"

"People can't hide that sort of thing." Celestial studied the scene out on the drive. Lord Westwood dropped his hand from Lady Harriet's waist immediately after she descended from the carriage steps. Both wore stony expressions. Emerging from another carriage were Heavenly, her pursed lips and arched brows pregnant with meaning, and a slightly older man—one of Lord Westwood's servants, perhaps—who looked as if someone had just died.

"Something momentous has occurred," Celestial said.

"What?"

Celestial's gaze narrowed thoughtfully. "She is returning without her father but with Lord Westwood. The duke wouldn't have released her without a reason, so I expect Lord Westwood means to marry her in earnest now. Perhaps they are already wed, since they traveled all this way in a closed carriage."

"I don't think so." Horace shook his head doubtfully.

"I do." Celestial clapped her hands together. "This would be an excellent time to tell them about us. Though we wed without Lady Harriet's permission, she could not possibly object now. Neither will Heavenly, what with Lady Harriet embracing happiness and her new love."

"That is not the face of a woman who has been embracing anything," Horace declared. "Or anyone."

Celestial peered at Lady Harriet, who was climbing the front steps slowly, as if the weight of the world sat on her shoulders.

Horace hurried to throw open the door. "My lady," he said, "welcome home."

Celestial could not hear Lady Harriet's response. But her mistress's tone told her that Horace was right—something was very, very wrong.

When Lord Westwood's servant carted his trunks into the house behind him, Celestial's eyes widened. So they *had* married! But Celestial had been married a week herself, and never once had she felt so downcast as Lady Harriet looked. Her mistress had obviously been forced into marriage, probably by that father of hers. Or by Lord Westwood, who was a forceful sort, too.

As Celestial hurried to the kitchen, she stole a look at the earl. He was studying Lady Harriet, and Celestial was surprised to see longing in his gaze. He cared for her!

Here was a chance for Lady Harriet to find the happiness she never had with Lord Worthington. But Lady Harriet was a stubborn woman. She would not submit to love easily. Lord Westwood would have his hands full trying to win her heart.

Perhaps, thought Celestial, he needed a little help.

Chapter Fifteen

"I still cannot believe that Monica and Cedric—" Harriet shook her head.

"I was a bit leery myself." Eustace shrugged. "But Gibbs seems a changed man. And Mother is happy."

Harriet thought Eustace must be a changed man as well. Gone were the stiff, impossibly high collars he favored earlier in the Season. Now his jacket molded to his lanky form with none of the sharp angles and exaggerated padding typical of the dandy set. His straight-legged trousers were far removed from the voluminous Cossacks that Monica had found so unattractive. Eustace now dressed very much like Lord Westwood, with understated but impeccable taste.

"I do hope you are right." Harriet did not want to think about her husband. It was enough that he sat across from her night after night, eating dinner as if everything were perfectly normal. Nervously, Harriet took another spoonful of turtle soup. She could not place the seasonings and made a mental note to ask Celestial about it. The taste was not off-putting, though it did not go with turtle. "I hope Cedric understands that he must follow my rules as to the use of the mill and distribution of the flour."

"Oh, he does," Eustace assured her. "Mother made certain of that before she agreed to go back to Sussex with him. He is very excited about some new grinding stone from the Continent. Says it will produce a better quality flour. That is why they are planning a wedding trip to the Rhine."

Harriet wished her friend all happiness, but she could not help but feel a little abandoned. With Eustace doing so well on his own, Monica's attention would turn to the eight motherless children who needed her. She would not have time to share Harriet's confidences.

Not that it was in Harriet's nature to discuss her troubles. A person had to be strong or risk spending all day with tears running down her face. But like her, Monica had had a faithless husband; over the years, kinship had grown from that common bond. Harriet treasured Monica's friendship.

Now Monica was happy. And Harriet was miserable.

Harriet took another sip of soup. No doubt about it, Celestial had erred in the seasoning. She waited for Lord Westwood to comment, for his palate was remarkable, but he had eaten his soup as if nothing were amiss. So intently did Harriet watch him that she almost jumped when his gaze met hers.

"Is something wrong?" he asked.

"No." *Yes. I do not wish to be living in this house with you, seeing your face every day, knowing that your chamber is next to mine. I do not wish to think about your kisses and know that you expect to share a bed with me and wonder why you do not so much as venture into my room at night—*

"Harriet?" His eyes were gentle, inquiring.

Harriet jumped. "Yes, my lord?"

"What is bothering you?"

Her gaze shot to Eustace, the only other occupant of the dining room. Thank goodness he was here to act as a buffer for such probing questions. But even as she formed the thought, Eustace placed his napkin on the table.

"Please excuse me," he said, rising. "I have an engagement elsewhere."

Harriet eyed Eustace suspiciously, but Lord Westwood merely wished him a pleasant evening, then returned his attention to her. "Go on, Harriet. I wish to know what is causing you distress."

Harriet took a deep breath. "This marriage, my lord. It is as much of a sham as our betrothal."

Her eyes were unreadable. "Please continue."

"In the week that we have lived in this house together," Harriet rushed on, "we do not converse in any meaningful fashion, nor can we sit in the same room together without there being a strained air between us. I find your presence stifling."

"I would never wish to stifle you, Harriet."

"Well, you are, my lord. I cannot tolerate this atmosphere of . . . unnaturalness."

He took a sip of wine. "What would make the atmosphere more natural, do you think?"

Harriet fanned herself. The dining room was uncommonly warm. "Perhaps it is simply that we are not used to living together. We are too . . . aware of each other."

"I am very aware of you, Harriet."

"Yes, well, I think it would be best if we just act like any other married couple and ignore each other—"

"Is that what married couples do?"

"Yes. Freddy and I had a tolerable arrangement," Harriet replied nervously. "Indeed, we got to where we scarcely noticed if the other was in the house."

"I do not want a tolerable arrangement. I want something more." He paused. "Much more."

Harriet closed her eyes. She had expected this. He had given her time, as he had said he would. Now that time was at an end. He meant to claim his husbandly rights. She would be forced to share that big bed with him, and—as with Freddy—all of her protestations would be as nothing in the face of his selfish demands.

Dear Lord—the silence between them was palpable.

Harriet could not bring herself to open her eyes and face that steady, knowing gaze. She had said she would not perform her wifely obligations, but she had not expected him to accept that. Not a man like Lord Westwood—she still could not call him by his given name, for he remained a stranger. She could fight him, but what was the use? He was strong, forceful, powerful, and dangerous. He evoked unfamiliar passions in her. In his hands, she would be like a well-kneaded dough—malleable and helpless to do anything but rise to the occasion.

Harriet waited. And still he did not speak. What was he planning? The silence was maddening.

Cautiously, she opened her eyes. He was gone! He had left the room, left her in a state of breathtaking suspense with her eyes closed and her expectations running amok.

Harriet stared at Lord Westwood's empty seat and the napkin he had placed neatly on the tablecloth before slipping away. Dazed, she speared a piece of turtle meat and put it into her mouth. Again, that strange taste.

What in the world was in the soup?

His wife meant to kill him with kindness. Elias regarded the tray of pastries she had set before him like the exquisite treasures they were. Harriet had been engaged in feverish culinary experimentation, channeling a vast amount of nervous energy into the production of dozens of cakes, cookies, pies, and other confections. Elias had no doubt that tonight's dessert would be an extravagant product of her imagination—another drunken trifle, perhaps, or the cheesecake she had recently adorned with a sculpture of blueberries, kumquats, and marzipan.

If he did not expire from overconsumption, he might die of unrequited lust. And no matter what she served him, his appetite would not be satisfied by the most exquisite of Harriet's pastries, only by the woman herself.

Unfortunately, she was trying to avoid him, to the point of exhausting herself in the kitchen night after night.

Sometimes she stopped long enough in the afternoon to take tea with him, though she was so tired that Celestial had to pour. The tea seemed to restore her. After one cup, she usually lost her look of embattled fatigue. After another, she would fan herself and complain about the heat. Elias attributed her erratic behavior to the nerves that beset both of them.

He had to bed his wife, and soon. Perhaps if he could remain patient, she would come to him. Perhaps if she gave him a chance to remove those blinders from her eyes, she would realize that she desired him as much as he desired her and that, moreover, they were superbly well matched.

To his surprise, for the first time in his life Elias truly yearned to settle down. His travels, as profitable as they had been, had also served as an excuse to flee the public humiliation he had suffered at Zephyr's hands. To be sure, his business still needed him—he had left things undone in Jamaica to come to England for what he had naively supposed to be the simple errand of recovering his shares. He would have to go back eventually, but now his heart was here—with Harriet.

Perhaps he would hire someone to act as his agent so that he did not need to travel so often. On the other hand, if Harriet persisted in refusing to recognize what was between them, he would welcome a long trip. They could not spend many weeks in their current state.

Night after night Elias had stared at the door between their rooms, knowing he could probably have her if he wished. But though Harriet might allow him to make love to her, she would never let him touch the person within that lovely shell. She would tolerate his touch but withhold herself, and he would hate that.

Elias did not want her tolerance. He wanted her anger,

her rage—whatever it took to show that she cared. And so he had vowed not to go to her. She must come to him; only then would he know that she wanted him enough to trust, that her heart was ready to love again.

Love. The word conjured vague memories of childhood, of being rocked by a hazy image who spoke in low murmurings and wore swirling skirts. Elias barely remembered his mother. After her death, his father had gone off to fight in Ireland, eventually dying on some sodden battlefield far away from home. Elias had been raised by servants and then sent away to school. When he entered the military, it was the closest thing to a family he had ever known. For most of his life, love had been an empty word.

He thought he loved Harriet. Certainly he lusted after her, but he also desired her mind, with its charming mixture of the practical and fanciful. And while her cooking was truly magical, it would not have mattered to him if she could not boil an egg. None of the specific qualities he liked in her accounted for why he felt the way he did. He supposed it might take a lifetime to understand.

If only she would grant him that. If only she would not flee to that kitchen every day and night. Sometimes he thought she was almost ready to let down the barriers. Then she would smile brightly and dash off again, leaving him with a plate full of pastries and a heart full of longing.

The door opened, and Harriet swooped in with the tea tray. Elias closed his eyes and prayed for patience.

"Thank you, Celestial." With a sigh, Harriet sank against the chair cushions. "I do not know how I would manage without my tea break."

"You've been working too hard, ma'am," Celestial murmured as she poured out the tea.

"I am almost satisfied with the new sourdough. I will

not rest until I have it just right." Harriet turned to Lord Westwood. "The Egyptians made a wondrous loaf with that flour Lady Hester sent," she told him brightly. "It is called—"

"Kamut," he replied wearily.

"Oh." Harriet's face fell. "I have mentioned it."

"Endlessly." He regarded her over the rim of his cup.

Nervously, Harriet sipped her tea, then frowned. "What have you done to the tea, Celestial? I had just gotten used to that new brew, and now you have gone back to the old way." She was not in a very good mood. These days, teatime was the only occasion she enjoyed, and now Celestial had ruined it.

"The old way?" Celestial examined Harriet's cup. She looked at Lord Westwood, who was staring at his own cup very strangely. "Here," Celestial said hastily, pouring Harriet another cup. "Try this."

"Much better." Harriet drank deeply. This was the way she liked it, with the intriguing aroma that somehow reminded her of the turtle soup Celestial had made. "It is uncommonly good, is it not, my lord?"

Lord Westwood did not respond. Neither did he drink. He put his cup carefully on the tray and stared at her. Celestial slipped from the room, closing the door behind her.

As her husband's gaze held hers, a slow warmth crept over Harriet, and the most delightful uneasiness invaded her stomach. She had noticed the feeling more and more lately. Her thoughts had grown strange, too, for she had the sudden, silly impulse to sit in his lap.

Harriet stifled a nervous laugh. She could not do that, of course. That would be too bold, and she would regret it almost immediately. And so she sat there, drinking her tea, fanning herself and smiling pleasantly at her husband.

Suddenly, he swore. Harriet's teacup halted midway to

her lips. Angrily, he plucked the cup out of her hands, sniffed it suspiciously, and almost threw it onto the tray.

"What are you doing?" Harriet demanded.

He muttered another oath. Then he pulled her to her feet and jerked her hard against him.

"This is ridiculous," he growled as he brought his lips to hers. And though they had lived such a polite, restrained existence for the entire tension-filled week of their marriage, there was nothing polite about this kiss. His mouth plundered hers like a marauding pirate, crushing her lips with a violent, shuddering passion and brooking no refusal as he bruised her swollen lips into compliance.

Harriet thought she might die from the thrill of that wondrously rampaging kiss. With a little sigh, she wrapped her arms around him.

And then, merciful heavens, she *was* sitting in his lap, and it was as if all the tension and strain between them had never been. It felt perfectly right to be with him on the sofa, his hands caressing her in wondrous discovery, as if she were a priceless treasure.

A feverish excitement gripped her. She ran her hands through his hair, savoring the way his tousled mane slipped through her fingers. Feeling very bold, Harriet pulled his face down and kissed him, her parted lips trembling with longing. Then, suddenly, she was lying on the sofa under him as he trailed slow, delicious kisses over every exposed inch of her tingling skin.

Her entire body ached for him. Her nerves quivered like the tightly wound strings of a musical instrument. She arched upward, desperate for his touch.

"Harriet," he rasped, "you are driving me mad."

"Yes," she said breathlessly. "That is how it is with me. Please, my lord. You must *do* something."

"Are you sure?" His gaze held a haunted look.

Harriet tried to think. It was all so strange, this desperate feeling inside, as frightening as it was compelling. Something had control of her, driving her onward, and it was not anything that could be denied.

His dark, mesmerizing eyes gleamed with promise, desire, danger. Yet he held himself back, keeping his full weight off her as he braced on his elbows to study her. Looking up at him, Harriet knew that this gentlemanly touching was not enough. She wanted to take every ounce of his weight, to feel all of him. This driving force within her would be satisfied with nothing less.

Recklessly, she reached for him, pulling him down to receive her helpless, yearning kiss. "Please," she moaned against his lips. *"Please."*

And suddenly her skirts were flying, and his hands were exploring, touching, caressing. They trailed over her ankles, her calves, her thighs, and then they touched her in that place Freddy had never even noticed, and Harriet was whimpering startled, embarrassing, shocking pleas she could not begin to keep to herself.

Her universe had suddenly shrunk, defined solely by that connection between his hand and her sensitive flesh. Urgency filled her. Burying her head in his shoulder, Harriet clutched him in helpless desperation. Her mind deserted her as raw, delicious pleasure held her captive. She heard herself begging, keening.

Then abruptly her world expanded, exploding in a thunderous tumult that washed over her and rippled to the far, far horizon. She cried out and knew she ought to be mortified by such a display, but she could do nothing other than let the unbearable pleasure take her to the stars.

At last, Harriet opened her eyes. Lord Westwood's face came slowly into focus. His riveted gaze, his sensual lips, his high, majestic cheekbones encompassed the whole of her existence. Marveling, she ran a finger along his jaw. Her thumb touched his lips, and he inhaled sharply. His searching eyes radiated beams of shimmering desire, along with something so breathtaking she could not identify it.

But even as she touched him, a new sound entered the periphery of her awareness. It was loud, insistent.

Someone was knocking on the parlor door. Lord Westwood ripped his gaze from her.

"Go away!" he barked.

"But there is a message, my lord," protested a familiar voice on the other side of the door.

"Later, Henry," he growled savagely.

From the hall there came a heavy silence, then a long-suffering sigh followed by departing footsteps. And though they were once more alone, the damage was done. Harriet blushed in shame.

"I am sorry," Lord Westwood murmured, but his stricken expression did not ease Harriet's embarrassment at the realization that she lay on the sofa in a shockingly exposed state after having just given free rein to the most primitive desires she had ever known. Mortified, she sat up and adjusted her skirts.

"It does not matter," she said stiffly.

His hand stilled hers. "It does."

"I do not know what came over me." Harriet shook off his hands. "Please excuse me, my lord. I must repair myself."

Fleeing like a frightened rabbit, Harriet made it all the way up the stairs without encountering anyone. When at last she gained her chamber, she threw herself on the bed in tears.

Horace did not much care for Henry, on account of the notes he had written that had caused the episode with Mr. Hunt and given Lady Harriet such distress. And though Horace was prepared to give Henry a chance to find his place in the household, the man had so far proven himself a bumbling menace. As butler, it was Horace's duty to set him straight.

"You ought not to have interrupted," Horace said sternly. The others nodded. Lady Harriet had retired for the evening, and Lord Westwood had gone out, so the servants were gathered at the kitchen table for a restorative glass of sherry. "A man and his wife are entitled to their privacy."

"They were in the parlor, for God's sakes," Henry protested. "How was I to know they might be, ah—" He broke off, reddening.

"Getting to know each other," Celestial finished, for she had spied her disheveled mistress fleeing from the parlor and knew exactly what sort of activity would cause such a state.

Horace cleared his throat, but before he could speak, Heavenly jabbed Henry's chest. "You have no sense of how it is between a man and wife."

Celestial and Horace exchanged glances. Heavenly had surprised them by keeping to herself whatever regrets or objections she had about her sister's marriage. Instead, she was concentrating on trying to make their mistress happy. All of them were. Only Henry remained recalcitrant, and Heavenly had mounted a one-woman campaign to reform him.

"You'll have to be more careful," Heavenly warned him. "Why, I brought her a tray in her room tonight, and she didn't eat a thing. It's all your fault!"

"It is not," Henry retorted. "Mr. Wilson's note was important. I was just trying to—"

"Nothing is more important than Miss Harriet's happiness," Heavenly snapped, grabbing Henry by the ear.

"Ouch!" He wrestled from her grasp. "Damned women. His lordship and I were perfectly happy before, when there were no women to mess things up."

"If you do not like it here, Henry, you are free to leave," snarled a cold voice.

The servants let out a collective gasp. Like a dark, avenging angel, Lord Westwood towered over them, his gaze murderous.

"Your lordship!" Aghast, Horace scrambled to attention. "We did not hear you come home."

Henry also jumped to his feet. "I beg your pardon, sir. I meant no disrespect."

Lord Westwood regarded him coolly. "We have been together a long time, Henry, but if you ever disturb my wife again or speak ill of her, I will turn you out of this house like a common thief."

Henry paled. "Yes, my lord."

"The same goes for anyone else in this room," Lord Westwood said. Then, to the amazement of all, he walked over to Celestial and fixed her with a hard gaze. "You will stop putting ginseng in my wife's food."

Horace gasped in shock. Heavenly's eyes grew wide.

"How did you know?" Celestial asked calmly.

"You will apologize to his lordship immediately!" Horace thundered to his wife. But she merely regarded their employer curiously, waiting for his response.

Lord Westwood held her gaze. "This afternoon you gave me Harriet's tea by mistake. I took a sip and immediately detected it. Later, I examined the new cup you gave her. It contained ginseng also."

"Your nose is uncommonly skilled." Celestial eyed him with rueful admiration. "Lady Harriet always said so."

"Celestial!" Horace stared at her, appalled at her cavalier treatment of what he viewed as a dire offense.

The earl's brows drew together. "I will not have my wife dosed like a—"

" 'Twas for her own good," Celestial interrupted defiantly. Horace buried his face in his hands. "She needed a bit of a nudge, that is all. The ginseng will stimulate her carnal appetites—"

"Good God," Horace muttered.

"—and give her extra energy as well." Celestial shot an affectionate glance at her husband. "Though not all of us need such stimulation, Miss Harriet is just a wee bit skittish. I am sure she will come around—"

"Silence!" Lord Westwood roared.

Celestial clamped her mouth shut.

"I am well aware of the reputed properties of ginseng." He spoke slowly, deliberately, as if striving for control. "I will brook no more interference. Do you understand?"

Warily, Celestial nodded.

Lord Westwood studied her for a long moment. Then his gaze moved to each of the others. "Anyone else who dares to meddle with my marriage will be turned out before he—or *she,*" he added, glaring at Celestial, "can say—"

"Napoleon?" she interjected helpfully.

The earl grew rigid. His fists clenched into tight balls at his side. He turned on his heel and strode from the room, pausing only to duck through the doorway.

Celestial looked supremely unconcerned. But at the sound of her husband's voice, she quickly turned.

"My dear," Horace said in a constricted tone, "I believe we have matters to discuss. You will come with me."

Because he prided himself on his manners, Horace waited calmly for her compliance. But he did not feel calm. No, indeed.

To everyone's surprise, Celestial rose meekly and followed him up to their room.

Chapter Sixteen

"Offer the man a tidy sum for his trouble," Elias told Jeremy Wilson. "Write him today and tell him to expect me at the end of August."

"But you would have to sail next week." The solicitor looked uncertain. "And, well . . . you have only been married a fortnight."

"The matter requires my personal attention," Elias returned curtly.

"Yes, my lord." The solicitor busied himself with his papers.

Elias suppressed a sigh. Jeremy was a good man. Doubtless he thought a newly married husband and wife wished to spend time together. But Jeremy did not know what life was like with Harriet. At this point, Jamaica seemed a godsend.

Elias had purchased the plantation in question a year ago, but an obscure relative of the former owner had recently surfaced to lay claim to the property. The man would probably be satisfied if Wilson sent him a token payment, but Elias had decided to see to the matter himself. It was time to return to Jamaica anyway. With a growing season that lasted virtually the entire year round, crops were always ready for export. Harvesting, shipping schedules, and new plantings had to be meticulously coordinated. Every day he put the trip off jeopardized his carefully constructed enterprise. He had to leave, and soon—especially given the state of his marriage.

The knowledge that he would soon put an ocean between himself and Harriet should have buoyed him, but by the time Elias reached his chamber, he was in a foul mood. "Brandy, Henry," he barked, flopping into a chair.

His batman quickly set a glass at his elbow. Lately, Henry had practically fallen over himself to please. Most employers would have discharged him after the Hunt affair, but Elias and Henry had spent more than a decade together, much of it risking their lives for their country. Over the years, Elias had developed a fondness for the rascal.

Knowing Henry's dislike of anything more than superficial involvement with the female sex, Elias suspected that he, too, was thoroughly miserable in his new surroundings, what with Heavenly and Celestial ruling the roost below stairs—and maybe above stairs as well. Then again, the high-handedness of Harriet's servants fit Henry's nature perfectly. A more meddling group Elias had never seen. He still grew furious when he thought of Celestial's scheme to dose Harriet with an aphrodisiac.

His wife would come to him of her own free will or not at all. More and more, though, it looked as if it would be not at all. Since that afternoon in the parlor, when she had obviously been under the heady influence of the ginseng, Harriet had studiously avoided him. Elias yearned to show her that she need not be ashamed of her passion, that there was so much more to discover between them.

But she had given him no chance. She avoided him at every turn. If he had to spend another meal with Harriet staring resolutely at the centerpiece, he would scream.

In frustration, Elias kicked at the footstool, sending it toppling onto its side. That made him feel like a quarrelsome child, and when Henry made a great fuss of righting the thing, Elias prayed for patience. He wanted nothing more than to be alone with his thoughts. But Henry refilled Elias's glass and stood at his elbow expectantly until Elias could no longer ignore him.

"What is it, Henry?" he growled.

Henry took a deep breath. "I have given the matter some thought, my lord. I would like to make amends."

"Amends?" Elias frowned. "For what?"

"Well, now that the deed is done—"

"The 'deed'?"

"The, er, marriage." Henry reddened. "Now that the marriage is accomplished, it would seem a pity for both parties to be miserable."

Elias regarded him in surprise. "Do I understand that you actually wish me happy?"

"I have always wished for your happiness, my lord," Henry replied stiffly. "I simply never trusted a female to provide it."

"I see." Elias pondered that point. Until recently, he had felt exactly the same. "Sometimes a man has no choice but to hope that she will."

Henry sniffed disdainfully. Elias eyed him curiously. "Have you never met a woman who left you no choice, Henry?"

The batman glowered. "Oh, yes. No choice about anything, even what to think. An incessant meddler, she is, always telling a man his business."

"A quality she shares with her sister." Elias had little difficulty surmising the identity of the female giving Henry such fits. "But Heavenly is a wise woman, too. I have even thought of employing her in my business."

"A *woman*? In business?" Henry looked horrified. "My lord, if a woman like that were allowed to conduct herself as a man's equal, she would run circles around him."

"Around the competition," Elias corrected dryly. "Perhaps she would leave us intact."

"*Us?* Oh, no, my lord. Do not involve me in anything having to do with that woman. She is a menace."

"Nice eyes, though—have you noticed?"

Henry stared at his employer. "I have *not* noticed the state of Miss Heavenly's eyes, or anything else about her person."

"No? Perhaps I was mistaken." Elias drained his glass and rose. "Do not wait up, Henry. I am going to my club, so as not to notice the state of my wife's eyes, or anything else about her person."

Frowning, Henry watched his employer saunter off down the hall. Lord Westwood was in an unsettled mood these days. Lady Harriet was to blame, of course, but Henry had decided not to hold that against her anymore. He had seen too much of war to realize when he was beaten.

The important thing was Lord Westwood's happiness. Unfortunately, that appeared to be entirely dependent on Lady Harriet, who seemed not to have the slightest idea how to be a wife. Henry had heard from the others that her first husband perished in the arms of his mistress. Had his wife known how to please him, Lord Worthington would not have strayed. Lady Harriet must have a great deal to learn about pleasing a man. Henry could not imagine why Lord Westwood wanted a woman whose deficiencies in that area had been so well demonstrated. But he did, and since Lord Westwood obviously did not have a clue how to win her over, Henry would have to help things along.

It would not be easy. Celestial's ginseng scheme had been well-meaning but flawed. Lady Harriet would have to come to her husband in a way that left him no doubt of the genuineness of her desire. She would need a nudge, perhaps, but an aphrodisiac was out of the question. The earl's inestimable nose would detect it right away.

What Henry knew about females would not have filled

Heavenly's darning thimble. But he did know one aphrodisiac that did not give off a scent, one so powerful that poets had found in it the stuff of a thousand passions.

Henry knew exactly how to make amends.

"What did you wish to serve tonight, ma'am?"

Harriet looked up from contemplation of the substance bubbling in several large tubs. "I have given it no thought, Celestial. Prepare whatever you wish."

"Certainly, ma'am." Celestial busied herself with the pantry. "Please let me know when you wish to resume setting the menus."

Other than this subtle reminder that Harriet was not herself, Celestial had been remarkably restrained in her comments. All the servants had, though they had probably guessed what had transpired on the parlor sofa. Harriet's face warmed just to think of it, and she could scarcely think of anything else.

Thank goodness she had her Egyptian sourdough culture, bubbling away in a state of happy ferment, for she could concentrate all of her efforts on bringing it up to snuff. This time the bread would be perfect—exquisite, even. Perhaps she would throw one of her parties to celebrate.

She did not feel like celebrating, though. Since that mortifying afternoon in the parlor, her husband had barely looked at her, whereas she found herself constantly staring at him. Every time she studied his long, tapered hands, she recalled how they had brought her such fierce pleasure.

Why had Freddy never touched her like that? A dreadful, unsettling, disloyal thought crept into her brain. For the first time, Harriet suspected that Freddy was as much to blame as she for the state of their marriage. Perhaps it was not her fault that Freddy had not wanted her. After all, Lord Westwood found her desirable, and he could have his pick of women.

It was a strange thought, that she was a desirable woman, but since that afternoon in the parlor, Harriet had been buffeted by strange notions. Every time Lord Westwood seated himself at the dining room table—the only occasion on which they were in the same room these days—Harriet wondered how it would feel to caress his broad shoulders without the barrier of that perfectly fitted jacket. Her mind's eye pictured him removing his jacket, his waistcoat, his shirt, his breeches, and then lying next to her, loving her in the way that he did in the parlor. Only this time, she would be able to touch him back in all those intimate places shielded by his clothes.

Such shameful thoughts! To avoid revealing them, Harriet had to keep her attention focused on the centerpiece. But in her room at night, Harriet stared at the door between their chambers with undisguised longing. Hearing him moving around in his room, Harriet tried to imagine the precise moment in which he removed his jacket, his shirt, his breeches. Did he wear a dressing gown, as Freddy had? Or did he sleep naked, stretching his long, muscled frame out on the bed like a lazy Greek god?

Harriet closed her eyes in helpless wonder. Now at last she knew the meaning of desire. She also knew she had never felt it for Freddy. Perhaps that is why she had tolerated his other "interests." It had hurt when the whole world knew that Freddy kept a mistress, when he paraded Caroline Forth about, making it clear that Harriet was not woman enough for him. But perhaps only her pride had been hurt, for she knew she had never truly wanted Freddy—not in the way she wanted Lord Westwood. Freddy had never sparked such uncontrollable desires.

How little she had known then—and only a few weeks ago, when she had forced Lord Westwood into that pretend betrothal. She had thought to understand the source of his masculine power, to arm herself against ever being hurt again. Instead, that very power had overwhelmed her. The closer she got to the source of desire, the more she realized it was unfathomable, frightening, delicious.

Would he make love to her again? He was gone so often at night she wondered whether he had taken a mistress. The thought of him with another woman shook her very being.

What would happen if she went to him and confessed the truth—that she desired him but feared losing herself? Would he laugh, as Freddy might have? Would he stare at her in puzzled disdain, the way her father always had when she tried to tell him that she wanted more from life than their lonely existence in Cornwall? Would he fail to understand her, as Freddy and her father had failed, leaving her hurt and determined to make her own way without men?

Was it possible to be a woman on her own terms and still lose herself in passion? She had always controlled her emotions and protected her innermost feelings. Now they were as unsettled as that bubbling sourdough culture.

"A bracing cup of tea would be just the thing," Harriet said, hoping her shaky voice did not betray the fragile hold she had on herself. "I wish you had not run out of that new blend. Can you get more?"

Celestial did not look up from the vegetables she was slicing. "The supplier is very unreliable."

Harriet added flour to the dough and began to mix it with her hands. "Can you locate a new supplier? I thought it a very special blend, well worth the effort to find more."

"Lady Harriet." Celestial put down her knife abruptly. "There is something about that tea you should know."

"Lord Westwood did not care for it, if that is what you

mean," Harriet said quickly, "but that is no reason to stop ordering it." She did not really want to talk about the tea, but she could not stop herself from babbling. "A husband and wife may have different tastes. I am sure you and Horace do not agree on everything."

"No," Celestial agreed ruefully. "We do not."

Harriet dumped the dough onto the counter. She had always loved this stage, the pushing and kneading of the dough until it grew smooth and elastic and satisfying under her hands. But today the process did not give her the usual pleasure. Instead, she felt a sudden urge to cry. She bit her lip and gave the dough a particularly rough turn. "I have always believed in tolerating differences."

Celestial eyed her warily.

"I would not wish to impose my tastes on Lord Westwood," Harriet continued in a wobbly voice. "I am sure he would not wish to impose his on me. Toleration is important in all things." With that, she burst into tears.

"Ma'am, what is wrong?" Celestial moved to her side.

Blindly, Harriet reached for a cloth to wipe her eyes. "N-n-nothing. My nerves are merely strained." She tried to smile. "What did you want to tell me about the tea?"

"Nothing, ma'am." Celestial gave her a hug so fierce it brought new tears to her eyes.

"Oh, Celestial!" Harriet sobbed. "I feel like the veriest fool."

"Now, now," Celestial murmured soothingly. "You need to get out. Horace is driving me over to Kensington later to fetch Heavenly from Mrs. Thornton's. Won't you come? Mrs. Thornton makes a delicious mutton pie."

"I-I do not know." In truth, Harriet wanted nothing more than to leave this house, which was heavy with the tension between her and Lord Westwood.

" 'Tis settled then," Celestial said firmly. "Now let's get to this bread. We will take Mrs. Thornton a loaf or two. It will be just the thing."

Harriet eyed the round ball of dough sitting placidly on the counter, unoffended by the rough treatment she had administered. Few things in life were more profound than the way dough was transformed by the blows sustained during its short existence. Without such a transformation, there would be no bread. The process of change was good.

Unless one left the dough too long to its own devices. Then it would rise too much, and the loaf would lose its substance. Wiping away her tears, Harriet wondered whether her own nature had undergone a bit too much leavening.

"What is it, Henry?" Deciding not to pass another empty evening at his club in the futile attempt to assuage his restlessness, Elias had immersed himself in the paperwork on his desk. He did not welcome the interruption.

"There is a lady to see you," the batman replied.

Elias frowned. "I am not expecting anyone. Have Horace send the caller away."

"Horace and Celestial drove with Lady Harriet to Kensington to fetch Miss Heavenly."

"The servants have more time off than I do," Elias grumbled, returning his attention to the papers. "Get rid of the woman, Henry."

"And what if I do not wish to leave?" purred a voice.

Elias's startled gaze shot to the door. Lady Caroline Forth stood at the threshold, eyeing him in frank anticipation, as if he were a well-seasoned pheasant.

"Lady Forth." He rose, wondering what the devil Freddy's former mistress was doing in his study. He turned to Henry, but his batman had slipped away—no doubt to watch the events through a keyhole somewhere.

"I have been waiting for the opportunity to congratulate you on your marriage." She moved into the room.

"When I learned that you were alone tonight, I knew that the timing was perfect."

"How did you know—"

"Pity that Harriet has left you to your own devices," she continued, pursing her lips in mock dismay. "Men must be carefully tended, especially in the early days of marriage when their needs are so . . . acute."

She pointed to the decanter on his desk. "May I?"

With a growing unease, Elias reached for a glass and poured Lady Forth some brandy.

"You do not join me?" Her voice held a note of reproach.

"I am working."

Choosing not to recognize the hint, Lady Forth let her shawl slide down to the crook of her arms. Her azure gown bared her shoulders and exposed rather a great deal of the rise of her breasts. The amusement in her gaze barely veiled a deeper, predatory gleam. Obviously, Lady Forth had not come merely to offer felicitations on his marriage.

Crossing his arms, Elias leaned back against the desk and waited. He did not have to wait long.

"Let us not play games, my lord," she said softly, moving closer. "I have thought of you since that night at Lady Symington's. Before that unfortunate interruption, when—"

"Harriet tossed that tree at us," he finished, arching a brow. "Yes, I imagine you would remember that."

She flushed, which Elias was certain she did not do often. "Harriet is a dear," she murmured, setting her glass down, "but there are things she does not understand."

"What things?" he growled, barely stifling an urge to toss the woman out on her lovely ear. Harriet's understanding certainly surpassed anything in Lady Forth's limited intellect. Anger at the pain Lady Forth had inflicted on her—with ample help from Freddy—surged through him. He wanted to put his fingers around her swanlike neck and strangle her.

"Harriet does not understand a man's appetites," she said in a velvety voice. "Can you honestly say that you are happy, my lord?" To his amazement and consternation, she took his hand and boldly brought it to her breast.

Elias studied the spot where his hand touched the rise of her soft flesh. He might as well have been touching a rag doll, for all the sensation she evoked in him.

"No," he said. "I have not been happy since the day I met Harriet." It was the truth. He would be eternally miserable until the barriers between them fell.

She nodded sympathetically. "Freddy felt the same. It is fortunate that I am here, Elias. You do not mind that I call you Elias?"

"You may call me anything you wish, Lady Forth."

"Caroline," she corrected, parting her lips.

Elias felt nothing for this beautiful woman who clearly understood the nature of lust and would have been just the sort to appeal to him not so very long ago. But the time when he might have entered into a dalliance with her was long since past. Only Harriet could assuage his unhappiness. Only Harriet could satisfy him now.

Gingerly, Elias tried to extricate his hand from Lady Forth's entwined fingers.

She refused to grant him his freedom. Capturing his hand in the valley between her breasts, she stood up on her toes, lowered her lashes, and touched her lips to his. It was a kiss like many he had shared over the years with countless women—flat, uninspiring, meaningless.

Nothing like Harriet's kisses.

When he did not respond, she kissed him more forcefully. With a breathless murmur, she pushed him back against the desk and pressed against him, letting their bodies touch most intimately.

"Good God, woman!" Elias protested, forcibly wrenching his hand from hers. "What the devil are you doing?"

"Now *that,* I think, is rather clear," came the very brittle voice of his wife.

Damnation. It wanted only this. With an inward groan, Elias looked over Lady Forth's shoulder to Harriet.

And quickly ducked. For in that precise instant, Harriet hurled something foul-smelling and sticky at them.

The stuff hit Lady Forth, who had her back to the door, just as she turned, bathing her elegant blue gown and heaving breasts in thick, stinking goo.

Chapter Seventeen

"Definitely more effective than a rubber tree," her husband observed, his unreadable gaze flicking from Harriet to Lady Forth and back again.

Though the sourdough culture had spared him, Caroline was virtually covered in it. Harriet wished her aim had been better; she had intended to douse them both. Even now, with Caroline's lovely features obscured by fermenting ooze, Harriet could not contain her rage. "How dare you?" she cried.

"Are you addressing me or Lady Forth?" To her astonishment, amusement danced in his eyes.

"Both of you! How dare you make love to that . . . that hussy in my house!"

" 'Tis my house, too," he said calmly. "Or had you forgotten our marriage?"

"*You* seem to have forgotten it, sir. I should have known that you would be like . . . like . . ."

"Freddy?" he offered.

"Yes! *Exactly* like that," Harriet declared. "A faithless, feckless frog of a husband!"

A wail had begun to emerge from the figure whose features were obscured by the thick white substance. The sound grew until at last it erupted in a loud, offended shriek. "I am *not* a hussy!" Caroline cried.

Harriet and Elias did not even look at her.

"A frog," he repeated in a musing tone. "A most unflattering comparison."

"You had no right to bring her here when you knew I might walk in at any moment."

"You are right, of course. I should have kept her out of sight in our secret love nest."

Caroline wiped her face on her silk skirt. "I demand a towel—get me a towel this instant!"

Harriet flushed. "You had no right to a love nest, secret or otherwise, my lord. You are my husband!"

"Ah, but do you not preach tolerance, madam?" he asked blandly. "Indeed, I thought it a tenet of yours."

"A *towel*!" Caroline shrieked. "I need a towel! What is wrong with you people?"

"The only tenet I have at the moment is an abhorrence of unfaithful husbands," Harriet retorted. "Please leave. And take your mistress with you."

His jaw tightened. "Lady Forth got herself here. She can see herself home. I am not going anywhere until this is resolved. You have formed a distinct misimpression—"

Caroline tugged on his sleeve. "But you sent your carriage for me, my lord. Had you forgotten?"

"*What?*" For the first time, he turned to her.

"Your note was so nice, so . . . poetic," Caroline added, sniffing. "I should have k-k-known that you were only trifling with my feelings." The wailing started anew. "Will someone *please* take me home?"

Harriet regarded him coldly. "Yes, do take her home, Elias. In your carriage. The one that you sent for her. Pity that the seats will be ruined by the mess, but there is nothing for it."

An arrested expression crossed his face. "You called me Elias."

"Oh, get out!" Harriet fled from the room, leaving her despicable husband to manage his smelly mistress. She hoped it took Caroline the rest of the night to get clean again. The woman deserved it.

After a while, Harriet heard the sound of carriage wheels, indicating Elias was taking Caroline home. Doubtless he would stay for hours, helping her cleanse her flawless body. Tears of hot anger spilled onto her cheeks. She could not block the image of that obscene embrace.

The drive to Kensington had improved her spirits immeasurably. Mrs. Thornton was a lovely woman, and Harriet had enjoyed the visit. Upon her return, she had been delighted to learn that Elias was at home. Feeling better than she had in days, she had gone to his study—just in time to witness him caressing Caroline's breast and confessing that his wife made him miserable.

Blind rage had driven her into the kitchen, where she had grabbed the first thing she found—the sourdough culture, bubbling happily, unaware that it was fated to ruin the gown of one of the loveliest Cyprians in England.

And now, though guilt should have plagued her, it did not. Her whole body still trembled with rage. Her head ached. She dared not let go of her fury for fear that despair would overtake her.

Like a restless cat, Harriet paced the length of her room. An hour passed. Elias did not return. Not even Heavenly came to her, though the servants must have heard the commotion. At midnight, Harriet heard Eustace come in and retire for the night.

Suddenly, an idea seized her. She could not stay here, waiting in vain for the return of the man who had betrayed her. She gathered a few things from her wardrobe, then slipped down the hall to Eustace's room. It took several knocks to rouse him, but finally he came to the door.

"Lady Harriet?" He sounded groggy, but his gaze

sharpened the moment he saw her face. "What is wrong?"

"I need you, Eustace. You must take me home."

"Home?" He looked confused. "But, you *are* home."

"To Sussex. Tonight."

He stared at her. *"Tonight?"*

"I cannot stay here." To her dismay, her voice broke.

Eustace held the candle up to study her face. "Has he hurt you?" he demanded grimly. "Have I mistaken his character after all?"

"He did not—"

"I will call him out," Eustace vowed, "even if he is your husband."

Touched by his fierce concern, Harriet shook her head. "He has not abused me, Eustace, but I cannot stay here. Please. I need you to—" But she could not continue. Like a frightened child she threw herself into his arms.

"Oh, dear," Eustace murmured in bewilderment. "Oh, dear."

"Henry!" Elias bellowed, though it was nearly three in the morning and the house was dark except for the brace of candles in the foyer. He was tired. It had taken forever to ferret out the truth behind Lady Forth's visit, for she had refused to speak with him until she had bathed and turned herself out in the style to which she was accustomed. He had spent nearly three hours at her house, most of them waiting in the parlor for her to come downstairs.

His batman emerged from the shadows. "Yes, my lord?"

Elias pulled out a paper and shook it in Henry's face. "You sent a note to Lady Forth in my name!" he roared.

Henry nodded. "Effective, wasn't it?"

"Effective," Elias repeated in disbelief. "Yes, Henry, it was damned effective." He held the note up to the candlelight and read: " 'Whenas in silks my Caroline goes, then, then (methinks) how sweetly flows that liquefaction of her clothes.' " He eyed Henry in disgust. "What revolting nonsense is that?"

Henry looked offended. "Herrick, my lord. The ladies love him. But that was just to soften her up. The part about the kiss is the best—'Give me a kiss, and to that kiss a score; then to that twenty, add a hundred more—' "

"Enough!" Elias thundered. "Why in God's name did you do it?"

From behind his back, Henry produced an open bottle of wine. Its fruity bouquet wafted through the foyer, and Elias involuntary registered the bottle as a superb French vintage. "Would you care for a glass?" Henry asked. "Lady Harriet keeps a fine wine cellar."

Elias advanced on the man. "I will kill you this time, Henry," he ground out. "Make no mistake about it."

"Wait, my lord!" Henry took a quick step backward. "From what I saw—er, *heard*—of tonight's little tiff, my scheme to bring Lady Harriet around worked to perfection."

With his hands mere inches from Henry's neck, Elias halted. "Explain yourself," he commanded.

"Old-fashioned jealousy, my lord—a better aphrodisiac than ginseng. Lady Harriet was as mad as a wet hen—she was ready to drown Lady Forth in that stuff. My plan worked beautifully."

Elias took a deep, calming breath. "Let me try to understand," he said slowly. "You sent flowery poetry and my carriage around to Lady Forth so that you could bring her here and make Lady Harriet jealous?"

Henry nodded, pleased at his employer's perceptiveness.

"And this jealousy was supposed to make Lady Harriet a willing wife—"

"In *all* senses of the word." Henry shot him a knowing

smile before he noticed the murderous rage in Elias's eyes. Instantly, he sobered.

With an outraged roar, Elias lunged for Henry—only to pull up short as a familiar voice said, "He should not have done it, my lord."

"Not at all," agreed another.

"But he meant well," said a third.

Slowly, Elias turned. Henry rolled his eyes heavenward in a grateful prayer.

"He only wanted your happiness, my lord," Heavenly said. At her side stood Celestial and Horace. "You cannot hold that against him."

"On the contrary," Elias said through gritted teeth. "I can."

"I think it worked," Heavenly added.

"You do?" Henry asked hopefully.

Heavenly nodded, and her gaze was filled with new respect for the batman. "First time I have ever known Miss Harriet to get angry quite like that."

"A very good sign," agreed Celestial.

"Normally, the mistress is never overset," Horace said. "But of course, we do not discuss such things," he quickly added, giving his wife a stern look.

Stunned, Elias glared at him. "I warned you, did I not?" he said softly. "You have intruded in my personal life for the last time. The whole lot of you are discharged this very moment."

They regarded him solemnly. "Lady Harriet would not like that," Heavenly said.

"Not at all," Celestial added. Henry eyed Elias reproachfully. Even Horace shook his head. "Not the thing, my lord."

Elias gave each of them a long, measuring look, but he knew when he was defeated. With a heavy sigh, he grabbed the wine bottle from Henry and poured himself a glass. To his chagrin, the servants instantly produced their own glasses. Elias arched a brow as Henry calmly poured them all wine. They drank in silence. The servants stared at him expectantly, as if waiting for the next chapter of this nocturnal adventure to unfold.

With a muttered curse, Elias drained his glass, set it on the table with a thump, and started up the stairs to find Harriet. When he was halfway up the staircase, Heavenly called out to him.

"She is not here."

Elias froze. "What?"

"She left about two hours ago with young Eustace," Horace confirmed.

"With *Eustace*?" Elias demanded, incredulous. "Where the devil did they go?"

"To Sussex, I believe," said Henry.

"After what she saw, you could hardly expect her to stay here," Celestial said indignantly.

"What she *saw*," Elias growled, "was a figment of Henry's misguided, impoverished imagination."

Henry shook his head. "I only copied the poem and sent the carriage, my lord. *You* kissed the woman."

"Tsk, tsk," Heavenly said reproachfully. "As if Miss Harriet hadn't put up with enough from Lord Worthington."

The worst thing about it was that they were right. Caroline Forth meant nothing to him; he should have tossed her out of his study immediately. Instead, he had let her throw herself at him. Why? Deep down, had he hoped Harriet would discover them together? Had he, too, put a modicum of faith in jealousy?

Then perhaps progress had been made after all. For though Harriet had disclaimed malicious intent in toppling the rubber tree, her purpose tonight in flinging that putrid mass at Lady Forth was clear. Harriet had abandoned tolerance. Perhaps jealousy *was* better than gingseng.

"Have my horse brought around," he ordered.

"Yes, my lord." With a jaunty salute, Henry hurried off.

"We should come, too," Celestial said. "We know her better than you."

"Celestial!" Horace admonished.

"She may be right." Heavenly eyed Elias skeptically. "How do we know you won't botch this one, too?"

Elias closed his eyes and prayed for patience. "You will all remain here," he said evenly.

"Of course we will," Horace assured him, his glare daring his wife to contradict him.

"I don't know . . ." Heavenly began.

"Heavenly!" Celestial said sharply. "Horace knows what is best."

The butler beamed.

Eustace had wanted to take her to Monica's cottage, but Harriet would not hear of it. She had lived in this house for years. She was very comfortable here.

Or so she had thought. They had arrived well after two, but though she was exhausted, the bed in her room was not as comfortable as she remembered. The house itself seemed unusually lonely. The few servants who remained behind when she removed to London treated her with polite deference, though her arrival had roused them from their beds. Heavenly would have given her an earful of complaints for interrupting her sleep. Harriet missed her cheering, intrusive familiarity.

Tossing and turning in that lonely bed, Harriet found her thoughts wandering painfully to Elias. She could not bear to think of him sharing the tender intimacies with Caroline that had made her own body sing with pleasure. His dalliance had hurt her in a way that Freddy's philandering had not. Her worst fears had come true. She had allowed a man inside her heart, and he had nearly destroyed it. And, foolish woman that she was, she still wanted him.

It was not even dawn. She had scarcely slept, but she was tired of lying in this lonely bed, envisioning Caroline and Elias together. Harriet sat up and threw her feet over the side of the bed. She would not become a helpless, lovesick woman. She had her own life, her own interests.

Dressing quickly, Harriet marched out to the stables. She harnessed her dappled gray to the gig and drove down to the village. It was Sunday, far too early for anyone to be about. She would have the shop to herself.

Making bread always calmed her. A woman at one with her dough had no reason to want for anything else. Bread was satisfying, reliable, faithful. Harriet did not bother to measure; her eyes and hands told her all she needed to know. When the dough was ready, she spread flour over the counter for the kneading.

And tried not to cry.

Dough was just flour and water and yeast. It did not fill her heart the way Elias did. Gazing out the window, Harriet felt the emptiness of years spent denying her feelings. She had made herself not care about Freddy. She could never do that with Elias.

But where did that leave her?

The sky had lightened, but her spirits were as heavy as lead. Dawn would soon give way to morning, and another day would lie endlessly ahead. She wished she knew what to do with it. One could not make bread all day.

Harriet pushed a strand of hair from her face, dipped her hands in flour, and resolutely reached for the dough.

Suddenly, the door swept open. It crashed against the wall like a clap of thunder. A figure ducked under the top of the door frame and advanced into the shop.

"Elias!" Harriet had forgotten how he dominated a room. Against her will, her heart turned a little somersault. "W-w-what do you want?"

"Whatever you are making." His dark eyes held turbulent seas that swept straight into her heart.

She tried to remember how to breathe. "I have not baked anything yet. I just arrived a little while ago, and I—" Harriet broke off. She was supposed to be angry at him—she *was* angry. But staring at him—her *husband*—she found it impossible to banish the sudden hope in her heart.

"I will wait." He moved toward the counter.

Harriet swallowed hard. Surely he did not mean to sit and watch her all morning. Her nerves could not stand it. His midnight eyes gave no hint of his thoughts, but Harriet suspected he meant to manipulate her somehow. Defiantly, she lifted her chin. "I shall not take you back, my lord, so it is no use even talking about it."

"You do not wish to share me with Lady Forth?" He crossed his arms and leaned back against the counter.

"Lady Forth is welcome to you," Harriet said coolly, hoping he did not hear the lie in her voice, "but I shall not tolerate a husband who plays me false."

"You have decided to throw the bounder out, then?" A burning intensity flickered in his gaze, then vanished, to be replaced by a strange, almost preternatural calm.

"Yes." Staring into that suddenly tranquil gaze, Harriet thought her heart might break. Except for that tragic flaw of infidelity, Elias was all she wanted in a husband: patient, gentle, loving, exciting—breathtakingly exciting. But while she had tolerated that flaw in Freddy, she now knew some things were too painful to tolerate.

He studied her for a long, breathless moment. "Would it matter if I said that I loved you?"

Harriet's heart thumped wildly, but she willed it to calm. "You cannot love me, my lord, or you would not have played me false."

"I did not play you false, Harriet."

She would not believe his pretty words. Harriet turned

away, unwilling to let him see the hope on her face. But Elias moved to her side, and she feared he saw everything.

"Henry wrote a florid note to Lady Forth in my name," he said quietly, "just as earlier he wrote those notes to you and Hunt. He sent my carriage to her. He was trying to make you jealous."

Jealous. Harriet wanted to laugh, the notion was so absurd. But the laughter on her lips died into a silent sob.

"He thought it would make you want me."

When had she not wanted him? Harriet lowered her lashes so he would not see the wanting in her. "I do not believe you. I saw you together."

"And you are certain of what you saw, are you not?"

She refused to hear the note in his voice that made her heart stand still. "I . . . do not know."

"Harriet." Gently, he put his hands on her shoulders and turned her around, forcing her to look into his eyes. There was pain in those dark depths, and—wonder of wonders—it mirrored her own.

"I did not kiss her," he rasped. "Not willingly, anyway. It was she who came to me, touched me. I know that sounds ridiculous. I do not expect you to believe me. I should have put a stop to it the moment she presented herself at the door." Now his gaze filled with regret and longing. "I love you, Harriet. Only you. There is no one else."

Angry tears welled in her eyes. How dare he play with her heart like this? How dare he stir the hope within her like a bitter stew destined only to be discarded?

With a sob, Harriet flailed at his chest, unleashing her outrage in a flurry of ineffective blows. He did not stop her, even when her flour-covered hands ruined his jacket. That he stood there, stoically accepting her impotent fury, made her heart break even more. Finally, in utter defeat, Harriet threw herself into his arms.

"I *was* jealous, Elias," she sobbed. "So very, very jealous. I have never felt this way before. I have always been so calm, so controlled. I do not understand."

"Harriet." He brought his lips to her ear. "Do you think it is possible that you might love me a little?"

She shook her head. "I will not!" she vowed through her tears. "I cannot. I am my own person, Elias. I will not be dependent upon a man for my happiness."

"You do not wish to be hurt. And I have hurt you more than you believed possible. Is that it?"

Harriet did not trust herself to speak. He brought her hands to his lips and softly kissed her fingertips. A bolt of desire shot through her. "I would like to try to change your mind," he murmured. "I would like to make love to you." He paused. "Now."

"Here?" she squeaked. "I do not think—"

"You are afraid to find out that you need me."

"I am not afraid." But she knew herself for a liar.

"Then you will not object to this." Slowly, he covered her lips with his. Helplessly, Harriet closed her eyes, savoring his touch. His kiss was gentle at first, then it erupted in a blaze of passion that was nothing less than a fierce battle for her soul.

"I hate you," Harriet murmured when he broke the kiss to nibble a tantalizing path down her neck. Another treacherous wave of pleasure shot through her, and she shivered in delight. "I hate you so very much."

Slowly, he removed the kerchief from her head. He smoothed her hair. "Stop fighting me, Harriet. I will not hurt you." Heedless of the flour on her clothes, he pulled her close and stroked her as if comforting a frightened child.

"You *have* hurt me," she sobbed into his chest. "When I thought that you and Caroline—oh, Elias! I will never, ever share you. You must not think that I will."

"No tolerance, then?" He kissed the top of her head. "No open mind on the subject?"

"None," she affirmed breathlessly as his hands slid slowly down her sides to her waist.

"Good." And before she realized what he was about, he lifted her onto the countertop. Now there was no more gentle stroking, only an urgency that would not be denied. Impatiently, his hands fumbled at the laces of her bodice, pushing the fabric aside so that he could touch her breasts.

Confronted by his desire, Harriet could no longer deny her own. Instinctively, her legs wrapped around him, pulling him closer. But her skirt bunched between them, preventing the contact she sought. Harriet gave a desperate little moan.

And in that moment she knew the battle was lost. The fight had gone out of her. She wanted only to surrender to the love that was in her heart.

Imprisoned within the circle of her legs, Elias stood perfectly still. Too still, she decided. Harriet removed his hand from her breast. Shards of loss shattered in his eyes. But in the next moment, loss gave way to wonder as she pushed her skirt out of the way and gently placed his hand on her bare leg.

He exhaled sharply. His fingers flexed on her skin, then slowly slid upward. In a moment they found that wondrous place he had brought to life that afternoon in the parlor. He held her gaze, and Harriet saw in his eyes the struggle for control.

"The counter is hard, and there is flour everywhere," he said in a constricted voice. "We do not have to—"

"Elias?"

"What?" he said hoarsely.

"I am quite accustomed to flour. It is all right."

His eyes held bottomless pools of desire. "It will be better than all right, Harriet."

"I know."

The sun rose over the village, shooting joyous rays through the window and bathing them in its blessed light. Harriet and Elias made love on the flour-covered countertop, and it was better than all right.

Chapter Eighteen

Heavenly, Celestial, Horace, and Henry arrived at Harriet's country home in time for breakfast. Henry drove the others in Elias's carriage, which he had taken the liberty of borrowing. Monica, Squire Gibbs, and Eustace pulled up minutes later. Thus there was quite an audience when Elias and Harriet, their wrinkled clothes dusted in white, drove up in the gig.

"Good God! Did you pummel each other with flour sacks?" Cedric demanded. He was none too pleased at being roused from his bed by Eustace, who had the strange misconception that Harriet could not look after herself. Eustace had been frantic after failing to find Harriet at home this morning and hearing from the servants that an agitated Lord Westwood had come looking for her. Cedric had no desire to tangle with the earl, but he had brought his pistol and sword nevertheless. Now he felt like a fool. Whatever Lady Harriet and Westwood had done to each other, his employer did not look as if she had minded.

Eustace was too taken aback by the couple's appearance to speak, but Monica's eyes widened. "Oh, dear!" she murmured. "Oh, dear, oh, dear."

"I told you he would botch things," Heavenly told Henry. Celestial and Horace exchanged a glance, but said nothing.

Helping Harriet down from the gig, Elias acknowledged the group with a curt nod, but all his thoughts were on his wife. She had said very little since they left the bakery. Indeed, she seemed to be in something of a daze. Did she have regrets? he wondered, his heart sinking.

He had none. Being with Harriet surpassed his wildest dreams. He only hoped he had not hurt her. Or shocked her. Or repulsed her. Though she had clung to him with wild, whimpering pleas, perhaps the memory of her behavior now embarrassed her. Elias cursed his own lack of control. Harriet deserved better than to be mauled on a flour-covered countertop.

At least he could protect her from the intrusive scrutiny of their nosy neighbors and servants. Barking an order for a bath, Elias hustled Harriet past seven pairs of curious eyes and up the stairs to her room.

Once inside her chamber, Elias's sense of mission faltered, however. Faced with the heavy, almost palpable silence between them, he could not think of a thing to say. Harriet, meanwhile, was looking everywhere but at him.

Fear gripped him. He had betrayed her trust by unleashing the whole of his desire upon her—when he had known that she was not comfortable with passion. Surely he was the last person she wanted to see right now. Excusing himself, he turned toward the door, his heart heavy with loss.

"Elias?"

He froze. His hand hovered just inches above the doorknob. Slowly, he turned, dreading the look in her eyes. He did not know how he would bear her regrets.

"Yes?" Their gazes locked. Her limpid blue eyes held uncertainty and a heartbreaking vulnerability.

"I was not a very good wife to Freddy. I would like to be a better one to you. But—" She broke off.

Elias's heart stuck in his throat. "Harriet," he began, anguish ripping through him. "I am sorry—"

"No—let me speak. Please." Shyly, she caught his

hand. "This morning I learned just how little I know about myself. And I learned how . . . how things can be between a husband and wife."

"It does not have to be like that," he rasped. "The counter was hard and uncomfortable. I should not have—"

"Oh, Elias!" With a little sob, she rushed into his arms. "You were right. I do love you a little. More than a little. Truly, I should die a thousand times over if you ever so much as look at Caroline Forth again. I am afraid I have become a wretchedly weak woman."

Harriet loved him.

Elias's spirits soared to the heavens. Burying his face in her silken hair, he savored the scents of yeast and flour that clung to her. He brushed a white spot from the tip of her nose. This was how she had looked the first time he saw her—rumpled and flour-dusted. The most lovable woman in the world, had he but seen it at the time.

"If you are weak, love, then I am weaker, for I no more have strength to stay away from you than I do to fly to the moon." He gazed deep into her eyes, willing her to see the truth—and the promise—of his love. "I shall never look at another woman, Harriet. You are all I could ever want." He paused. "Freddy was out of his blasted mind."

Her blessed, beautiful laughter made his heart sing. "Oh, Elias," she said, smiling through her tears, "you make it seem all right that I have abandoned my independence—"

"Stop." He stemmed the flow of her words with a kiss, immersing himself in the universe of those soft, ripe lips. But he knew he could not let lust rule this time. This was too important.

Reluctantly, Elias severed the kiss. He looked down into her eyes, eyes that held such wondrous promises of their own. "I do not expect you to change just because you have fallen in love."

She blinked. "You do not?"

"What I want is you. Nothing more, nothing less."

She pondered that. "I do not want to give up the things I enjoy," she confessed. "Why, I even thought someday I would travel the world like Lady Hester."

"Then you shall do so," he replied.

She studied him. "I am excessively fond of my salons."

Elias scowled. "I suppose you would wish to invite Oliver Hunt."

"I am not sure Mr. Hunt would wish to come again, but he does have many stimulating notions."

"Just as long as they are not *too* stimulating." Elias pulled her close. But as he bent his head to claim her lips, she pushed him gently away.

"And the bakery?" she prodded anxiously. "Do you still regard it as inappropriate?"

Elias was suddenly very aware of his nose. The scent of their lovemaking was still on both of them, and it mingled with the flour and yeast and filled the air around them with all manner of delicious smells.

"My attitude toward the bakery," he said carefully, "has undergone a radical change."

"It has?"

"Most definitely." Elias yearned to make love to her again. But it was too soon, he told himself. Her flour-laden clothes must be uncomfortable. She would want a bath, perhaps a rest. She would not want him, not now, not yet. He nuzzled her neck anyway.

"Then you did not really mean to reform me?" Her voice caught on a low, husky note.

"Yes, I did," Elias confessed, trying to stave off his body's increasingly urgent response to her. "But instead, *I* changed. I fell in love with you."

"Oh, Elias!" Harriet threw her arms around his neck, stood up on her toes, and parted her lips for his kiss.

His scruples flew out the window. If Harriet did not

think it too soon to make love again, he was not about to argue otherwise. He kissed her, and as she melted willingly into him, he wanted only to brand her with his love.

They tore at each other's clothes. She pulled off his jacket and waistcoat, then fumbled with his shirt laces. When her hands at last touched his bare chest, she sighed happily.

"I am glad you do not wish to change things," she murmured, nibbling at his skin. Her tongue found one of his nipples, and Elias shuddered with desire. With a primitive growl, he picked her up and headed toward the bed.

A loud, urgent knock sounded on the door. In the next instant it swung open. Horace stood at the threshold, holding a large copper tub. Celestial, Heavenly, and Henry crowded around him, each carrying kettles of hot water.

"Your bath, madam," Horace intoned.

Though Horace kept his face a careful blank, the others were not so circumspect. They stared openly at Elias's bare chest and Harriet, captive in his arms with her rumpled skirts exposing rather much of her legs.

"See?" Celestial nudged her sister. "I told you. Nothing to worry about."

Heavenly eyed the rippling muscles of Elias's bare arms. "I don't know," she said dubiously. "He is awfully large, isn't he?"

"Lord Westwood wouldn't hurt her," Henry insisted. "Why, look at them—smelling of April and May. Don't wonder if there isn't a little one crawling around this time next year—"

With a savage curse, Elias kicked the door shut. It slammed resoundingly in Henry's face. "There are still a few things around here I mean to change," he growled.

"Whatever you say, Elias." Harriet smiled. "But do try to keep an open mind."

He made a low, exasperated sound. "You are the most frustrating woman I have ever met—"

"Thank you for understanding me." She kissed him with all the love in her heart, and Elias thought his knees would buckle from the force of his love for her. Wordlessly, he carried her to the bed.

A long time later, Harriet looked at the man sleeping next to her and thought of a change *she* wished to make. It had to do with those delicious pastries she had concocted, the ones with the delectable cream filling.

Napoleon was a silly name. Who would want to eat a dessert that recalled a villain who wreaked havoc over two continents? From now on they would be eliases, in tribute to the man she loved, whose sensual appetites were perfectly captured in those decadent confections. She would serve them at her salons. The name would be sure to catch on. No doubt eliases would soon be all the rage.

"Eliases," she murmured happily, rolling the name around on her tongue. "Yes, that is perfect. Like you."

"What?" he answered sleepily.

"Never mind."

Elias opened one eye. Groggily, he pulled her into his arms. And there she remained, spinning recipes for love.

Epilogue

"I told you everything would turn out for the best," Celestial said. "With Miss Harriet's way with food and Lord Westwood's—what is that word you used, Horace?"

"Olfactory," the butler pronounced proudly, for he had worked hard to improve his reading and vocabulary.

"Lord Westwood's olfactory skills," she continued, "their business will be a wonderful success."

Heavenly frowned. "I don't know if I want to travel all that distance. Jamaica is such a far place."

"Nonsense." Celestial pulled a loaf of bread from the oven and turned it out on the counter to cool. "You will love it there. With Miss Harriet's baby due soon, they will need you more than ever. Besides—if the duke can make the journey, anyone can."

Horace nodded. "The duke is a new man these days. I think he is hoping for a granddaughter."

Heavenly regarded her sister uncertainly. "It would be so much better if you were going."

"I shall miss you, dear, but in my condition, I cannot travel. Dr. Stinton says I may be carrying twins. Besides, Horace rather likes Sussex. And someone must keep the bakery going until Lady Harriet returns."

"Mrs. Tanks . . . Gibbs would do so," Heavenly pointed out. "Now that Eustace and the children are helping with the mill, she has more time."

"Mrs. Gibbs does not understand the dough," Celestial

replied. "Cheer up, sister. You will have Henry to keep you company."

Blushing, Heavenly looked away. "I cannot imagine traveling such a long distance with that infuriating man."

"Henry's heart is in the right place," Celestial said, "but he has a lifetime of bachelorhood to overcome. I would not be surprised if a long sea voyage is just the thing to accomplish that."

"I have no intention of—"

"Take this." Celestial set a small vial on the table.

"Celestial," Horace warned, "you are not to interfere in that man's life."

"What is it?" Heavenly stared at the little bottle.

"Ginseng." Celestial gave her a sly smile.

Heavenly lifted her chin. "If a man doesn't want me on his own," she said huffily, "I'm not going to slip something in his ale to change his mind."

"Oh, it is not for Henry," Celestial replied. "I have little doubt where his inclinations lie. It is for you."

"What!"

Celestial sighed. "If anyone needs a nudge, 'tis you, sister. Otherwise, you'd never admit that you want him. And he won't approach you; he's too proud—and wary."

Horace gave a wise nod. "A man won't venture down an unfamiliar road when it's strewn with thorns that could tear him apart."

"*Thorns?* Are you referring to *me,* Horace?" Heavenly drew herself up. "There is nothing thorny about me." Celestial and Horace rolled their eyes.

Heavenly stared at the little bottle of ginseng. She had never had much faith in Celestial's quackery, but her sister was right about one thing: Henry had been on her mind for days. Living in the same house with him was driving her mad. But he would never approach her. Celestial was right about that, too.

It would have to be up to her. And she was never one

to rely on false courage. Eyeing the bottle disdainfully, Heavenly left it on the table and strode out of the kitchen to find Henry.

They stared after her. "What do you think will happen?" Horace asked.

Celestial handed him a slab of freshly baked bread. It was still warm. "What will," she said softly. "Here. Try Miss Harriet's new sourdough recipe. It is just right."

Horace took a bite. "Mmmm," he murmured, pulling his wife into his lap, "perfection."

Author's Note

Harriet's eliases may not have caught on, but napole-ons certainly did—though not until the late nineteenth century. Some food historians think the pastry was named not for Napoleon Bonaparte but for Italy's famed Neapolitan bakers. The confection itself is in-disputably French, however. As far back as 1758, a Frenchman published a recipe for "*mille-feuille*" ("a thousand leaves"), a sweet cake with five or six layers of puff pastry and pastry cream.

Which is exactly how Harriet envisioned them.